Jean Buffong is a Grenadian who has lived in England since 1962. Her novella, *Jump-Up-and-Kiss-Me*, was published together with Nellie Payne's *A Grenadian Childhood* in the popular *Jump-Up-and-Kiss-Me: Two Stories from Grenada* (The Women's Press, 1990). Her first solo novel, *Under the Silk Cotton Tree*, was published two years later to great acclaim (The Women's Press, 1992); and *Snowflakes in the Sun* is her third book.

Snowflakes
in the Sun

JEAN BUFFONG

First published by The Women's Press Ltd, 1995
A member of the Namara Group
34 Great Sutton Street, London EC1V 0DX

British Library Cataloguing-in-Publication Data
A catalogue record for this book is available from the British Library

ISBN 0 7043 4423 8

Photytypeset in Bembo by Intype, London
Printed and bound in Great Britain by
BPC Paperbacks Ltd, Aylesbury, Bucks

Dedicated to my children Michael, Angus and Caroline

Footprints on two shores

Memories

Remembering things of long ago
Of yesterday and of the days before.

Remembering the past
buried in deepest vaults
things preferred unremembered;

Memories
Remembering things we do not remember knowing
joy and pain
sorrow and laughter.

Memories
Listening
Listen to the memories.

1

'England eh, Lord that is a place.'

Uncle Dolphus sat on the sloping trunk of the coconut tree gazing across the marginless boundary of the horizon. The tiny waves rippled and bobbed along and around as they played hide and seek with the fishing boats that decorated the seascape. He shaded his eyes as he tried to distinguish waves from boats.

It was very early in the day. The gentle morning sea breeze seemed to prepare the land for the oncoming sunrays. Soon the large cruisers would be on their way from their night-sleeping anchor to the other islands.

The hands on the clock moved towards seven o'clock yet already nature's life was active. The sun was already saying goodbye to the mountainside on its journey across the sky to the horizon. The sky still partly clothed in fragments of stubborn breakaway clouds that lingered about like white decoration. Day life had taken over from night people. Butter-flies danced among the flowers, replacing the crickets. Birds were busily performing their morning duties, floating, dancing and singing among the trees, while the bees carried on polli-nating.

'England, heh England,' Uncle Dolphus muttered to himself again. His mind drifted across the oceans, contemplating time.

His thoughts wandered. He shook his head. A smile crossed his ruggedly tanned face.

The night before me and Aunt Sarh, she is Uncle Dolphus wife, went to look for cousin Nora. Funny how people become your family, you know. Uncle Dolphus is not really in our blood but because he married to Aunt Sarh, who is my mother older sister, we all look on him as our real uncle. Since they came home from England is Aunt Sarh and Uncle Dolphus to all the family and others. Another thing since they came down I spend more time at their house than I do at home. Mammy says she will put a big notice in the gap of our house saying 'DOROTHY MITCHELL does not live here anymore; try at Sarh and Adolphus Powell.' She says I spend so much time with them that I started repeating their England stories as if I'd been in England. Anyway, as I said, the night before we went to look for cousin Nora because Aunt Sarh said one of the children told her that the old lady was not well. We didn't go to stay late but when cousin Nora and Aunt Sarh start to beat mouth nothing could stop them. It was late when we got back so I decided to spend the night. The next morning I left the house to go and break some bush broom. As I turned the corner by the big flamboyant tree in the boundary with Mr Johnson on the bottom side I saw Uncle Dolphus sitting on the coconut tree trunk. He love that tree! He sit down there talking to himself loud loud as if is somebody he talking to. The way he shaking his head like he trying to get rid of the snow under his skull, as he usually says.

I break the bundle of broom, then look to see if the pawpaw tree had any ripe ones. I pick one big soursop to make some babalay. I then cut back by the side track under the house to clean out the fowl coop.

'England,' Uncle Dolphus repeated, his face reflecting distant thoughts. 'Lord that place cold. It make so cold; only snow and fog, snow and fog. That place cold even your blood in your body cold.' Again he shook his head as if shaking off the snow that soaked inside.

Bow wow wow bow wow wow, Bingo barked a few yards from where the old man sat. Bow wow wow, the barking continued. The sound of the dog brought Uncle Dolphus back to the present.

'Bingo. Bingo what's the matter eh, what's the matter?' He gazed in the direction of the barking dog. 'What noise you making dey so eh, behave yourself.'

The dog continued its insistent barking. Uncle Dolphus got up and went to investigate. His eyes strained in towards where he had tied the mother goat with her young ones. 'This damn goat; this blasted goat,' he mumbled, seeing the reason for Bingo's alarm.

Earlier he had tied Mamaanne under the shade of the big breadfruit tree overlooking the beach. The tree served as a boundary mark between his property and Mr Anson's. The mother goat had broken loose and was nibbling at pebbles on the shore, moving along the beach into Mr Anson's land. Uncle Dolphus hurried towards the animal.

'That damn animal; that blasted goat,' he continued to abuse the animal. 'If she not careful she go lose these kids. She will lead them straight in the water. She must think kids can swim. I tied Mamaanne where there is enough grass for she and the kids she so blasted stubborn. Is a good thing Bingo watching. Is a good thing he see her before she reach into Mr Anson land. That man so ignorant . . . he so ignorant . . . any animal mash his land they ready for the pot . . . just so he always saying he cutlass ready for them.

Uncle Dolphus crossed the small ravine that ran through the land. In the dry season that ravine was a godsend. The

3

only time it ever dried up completely was during the Lenten season. It served as a watering place for the animals and plants. Where the ravine had sprung from or even how it continued to exist, nobody knew; it seemed to have its source on the other side of the low mountain that ran between the village and the nearest town. Somehow nature had bitract that branch of the river through and over the hills and finally through Uncle Dolphus's property before it emptied into the sea.

'Baaa baaaa baaae,' Mamaanne greeted Uncle Dolphus.

'Baaa baaa,' the two kids joined her.

'Hee haw hee haw,' the donkey decided to call too, not to be left out.

The sun slowly drifted across the sky. Uncle Dolphus's merino was saturated with sweat as he recovered the animal. He decided to tie her under the avocado tree behind the bedroom window instead of returning her to her original position. As he tended the animal he talked to her.

'You is a bad woman Mamaanne, a wicked woman. You children could well fall in the sea. You know they can't swim. You is a bad woman, you hear me, a wicked woman.'

The black and white kid came and nuzzled Uncle Dolphus's trouser leg. He stroked her gently across her back. 'You mother is a stubborn woman, she is a bad mother,' he informed the kid. Then he laughed aloud. A deep, loud, hearty, throaty laugh like when he and his friends were sharing jokes.

'Bunjay these animals have me talking to them like that man in England used to talk to his plants. Big big prince you know. Man with high education spending his time talking to the plants in his garden saying when he talk to them they grow better. I planting garden since I a little child I never hear that. I think with all his money and education too much snow get under his skull.'

4

Uncle Dolphus carried on his one-sided conversation, the animals, birds and bees his listeners. 'Snow! Lord that thing fall on my head already oui, snow fall on that poor head you know. These people in this place see you come home to spend your last few days the Lord might let you live they think you had shares in the money mint in England. They don't know is lucky you lucky otherwise you bones left six feet under the snow. If I did follow Sarh I would of left that place long long time. Never mind nothing happens before its time. Since we meet up everyday she crying she want to go back to her country before she close her eyes. Everyday she want to come back on the piece of rock especially when the snow burn her feet and fingers. Was me that kept on saying let us hold on for our pension. Chupes – pension. What pension? The two pence they sending us by the time they change it to Eastern Caribbean dollars is nothing . . . nothing. Is a good thing I can still plant two banana stool and a hole of yam. Thank God snow didn't bite out my fingers.'

He stood under the shade of the tree and looked around at his garden. The banana plants were always producing. Yams, dasheen, pease; when they were in season he reaped handsome crops. He gazed lazily from one boundary to the other. He was contented. He was in no hurry. His hurrying days were over. He had settled to a slow leisurely pattern since returning to the island. Slowly he made his way back to the coconut tree where he'd been sitting earlier. On his way he cut a stalk of sugar cane, cut it into small joints and chewed them. He gazed out towards the ocean. The fishermen and their fishing tools would soon be settled there, plying their trade. Other sights had taken their places. Two large, silvery-white cruisers, chimneys belching thick greyish-white smoke, laid claim to the ocean bed.

The old man sat on the coconut tree trunk, thoughts

5

moving with the movement of the cruisers. His face was tanned like well-preserved leather, the deep ripples across it like a natural history book. His body was thin and wiry like the flex of a coconut leaf, his shoulders slightly hunched, he once said from carrying too many bags of snow. He watched the cruisers go by. His mind drifted. In 1958 he boarded an ocean liner that took him, a young man in the prime of his life to an unknown land, a land alien to him as the moon, a land he was taught was the motherland. He boarded a liner for the unknown. The only thing the liner and the cruisers that now meandered across the waters of the Caribbean had in common were their size. The meandering cruisers were pleasure grounds, not ships taking young men and women from their native shores to a foreign land to be called immigrants and most often to be treated second-class.

Those days long ago on board the ocean liners conditions had not always been good. Uncle Dolphus remembered how he spent his time during the journey. He had learnt from the crew things about that strange country where a bright sun was not necessarily a hot sun, the country that whenever cousins and friends wrote back home about was always painted in rosy glossy pictures. He learnt things from the crew that were never written about back home. He recalled generous women on board. Some he would of liked to keep in touch with; or others he was glad to say goodbye to at the journey's end. Memories of that journey were now only shadows in the pit of the old man's brain. He sat quietly, gaze fixed on the horizon.

'Dolphus; Dolphus oye; come come you tea ready,' Aunt Sarh called from the kitchen window. 'Aye aye since morning you down there is time for you to eat. You must hungry; come come.'

His wife's voice sounded like a whisper in the wind. He

heard but pretended he did not hear. He was not hungry. The cup of black sage he had earlier and the sugar cane satisfied him, but he knew his wife. He expected her to call again.

'Aaaye, Dolphus, the tea getting cold, come and drink it nuh. Come come I want to go in town. I want to catch "One More Time" when he doing the second trip. Dolphus you hear me? I want to clean up before I go.'

Uncle Dolphus got up, braced his cutlass under his arm and sighed heavily. 'That woman eh, that woman. I don't know what she put in town so. Everyday everyday she in town. I don't know what she have to buy so. Just spending the little money as it come in. The little pension they sending down for us don't worth nothing, nothing. If is not the two little things we selling things would of been worse for us.' Uncle Dolphus set off on one of his one-man conversations. 'I wish sometimes when she go in town she'll take a bag of coconut or a bunch of banana to sell. Lord what I saying? I don't want my wife go selling in market. I must be going crazy or something.'

He made his way slowly to the house. As he reached the yellow plum tree just under the kitchen window he looked up. His eyes clashed with Aunt Sarh's.

'I coming,' he said. 'Cover the tea with a towel and go where you going. I just suck a piece of cane, I all right.'

'You suck a piece of cane!' Aunt Sarh exclaimed. 'Piece of cane! Dolphus sometimes I wonder if you all right in your head you know. You know how gas does full you up if you don't eat in time you come telling me you suck piece of cane . . . chupes. You go on like a little child sometimes.' Aunt Sarh was really upset.

'Sarh why you don't go where you going? I tell you leave the tea I'll drink it when I ready. I coming, I just fulling the

7

pig pan with some water. The little ones drinking for so. They getting fat.'

He went to the pig pen, filled two old basins with water from a large drum and placed them where the pigs could reach. As he put down the basins someone called from the main road.

'Mr Dolphus, morning. Morning Miss Dolphus. Howdy neighbour howdy.'

'Morning Miss Almaoo, morning. How you this morning?' Uncle Dolphus acknowledged his neighbour's greeting.

'I dey so so nuh . . . so so. I waiting for a bus to go up by my sister in Grenville to come back. She daughter, the one I tell Miss Dolphus about the other day that was in the hospital, she out but she not well at all at all. My sister send message for me yesterday. My niece not good at all. She getting up in the middle of the night saying people calling her down by the Paradise River. All she on about is the man she have the child for calling her. She on about he have the child with him and they calling her. But Mr Dolphus she lost the baby. She never had the child, and the old nasty man gone in America. He not even writing her a line. Nobody could tell her the man done send for the woman he had in Grand Anse and married in America. She not well already when she hear that is straight in Richmond Hill she gone. I going and see what I could do. I don't know. I don't know what to say.'

While she talked Uncle Dolphus had joined his neighbour in the road. 'People, people, Miss Alma you have to be so careful. Some people you see them walking and talking nice and respectable but I tell you they don't wash their hands. You have to be careful. Is wash they wash hand on your niece. Is do they do her.'

'I know Mr Dolphus, I know but my sister don't want to hear that. I tell her to get Miss Isabella up in Mamacaan

8

to give the girl a bath but she don't want to hear me. She on about how all these things belong to the devil and she not having anything to do with that.'

'Is the devil work oui, but sometimes you have to use the devil work to cut the devil work. You know what I mean? Some work stronger than the other. Even if you don't believe in it you still see it in front you. Quite in England I know people used to dip their hands in that nastiness.'

'In England! Bunjay; you mean in England they believe in these things too? I didn't know that white people had hand in these kind of thing. Aaaaye I wouldn't think they know about these things at all.'

'Nuh not the white people. They believe in darkness too but they call it something else . . . sometimes white magic, sometimes black magic. I not talking about white people; is we own black people I talking about. Quite in England they practising their nastiness.'

'Miss Almaoo morning morning,' Aunt Sarh called to her neighbour.

'Aye aye Miss Dolphus morning. I call you but you inside you didn't hear. I just running up in Grenville by my sister.'

'O hoye you going by your sister,' Aunt Sarh came out on the verandah facing the road where she could see her husband and her neighbour. 'How you niece? She better?'

'Better! She not better. I was just telling Mr Dolphus as if is do they do the girl. I doh know. She on about how she hearing people calling her in the middle of the night and getting up to go outside. As soon as she get the chance is Paradise River she heading for.'

'Bunjay. Lord you all have to pray for her Miss Alma. Do some strong praying.'

'Prayer Miss Dolphus. I don't think prayers could do anything. When people work their nastiness on you, you have to

9

find somebody stronger to cut it. People bad oui, they bad oui aaaye. My niece never do nobody nothing. She never hurt nobody you know Mr Dolphus. Nice young girl, just so they want to spoil her. People bad oui.'

'If people bad!' Uncle Dolphus echoed. 'Sarh I just telling Miss Alma how black people bring their dirty hand all in England.'

'You telling me. England have its own nastiness but we people bring we thing with us too,' Aunt Sarh took over the conversation. 'Dolphus you remember that nice young girl that used to live in the back room in the attic when we was in Barnsbury Street?'

'The one that had the African boyfriend first time, then left him for that Jamaican man? I think she was from Guyana.'

'She self. Nice young girl about same age as Miss Alma niece. That was a thing you know Miss Alma, Dolphus could tell you. The girl used to work at Sainsbury's in Chapel Market in the day and in the evenings go to school to get she certificate to better herself. When she moved in she had this African boy. I think she said he was from Nigeria or somewhere like that. He was a ver mannersable young man. He never pass me without saying howdy. I thought they were going good. Then after a time I don't see him. I started seeing this big strapped man pulling up his car and going upstairs. I didn't know what was going on. Was Mary the Irish woman who was living in the front basement room with a Jamaican man that pinch me what going on. The man old could be the girl father.'

'I don't know why the girl didn't stay with the African boy. I don't know what she was doing with that man.' Uncle Dolphus added. 'As Sarh say, she could be his daughter. She was too young for him.'

'Is man. They the same all over the world. Anything nice

and young they after it. Is so God make them.' Miss Alma made the statement as though talking from experience.

'So God make them eh. To cause nothing but trouble. To spoil people children and then turn their back. He had his wife and still fooling around the girl. Next thing somebody go and tell his wife.'

'Bunjay. That is trouble self. Trouble self self. If the wife don't know is bad and not bad but . . . Lord. And Miss Dolphus I hear these Jamaican woman and them not easy you know. I hear they not easy at all. That man who used to work in the drug store in town his wife from Jamaica. I hear she worse than guinea pepper. I hear a time he playing man and started running behind a woman in Grenville and the news reached the wife. Nobody really know what happened but he couldn't work for months.

'She like that woman I used to work with in the Royal Free Hospital called Miss Godson. You remember her Dolphus? We used to meet she and her husband in the market every Friday evening. Miss Godson say anybody fooling around with her husband, when she ready to fight she making sure she take off her panty fold it up and put it aside in a safe place because when she finished fighting she don't want no tear-up panty on her. She was something. When people fooling around with other woman husband is trouble they asking for. Look what happen to that girl, nice young girl. Was Irish Mary that used to tell me what was going on. Mary was a nice woman.

'Perhaps because she was with a black man. She was one of the few white people I used to talk to without being too careful. I still watched my tongue because just as she used to tell me other people's business so she could take my business and spread it too, so I was always careful. Anyway, talking about that young girl, when she first came to live in the house

11

she used to look after herself. Then after a while I noticed when I saw her on the step or outside that the clothes on her old and hang up, hang up on her. Sometimes she talking and laughing to herself loud loud. One day I told Dolphus that that girl is going out of her head. A thing she used to do was go about knocking on everybody door asking for the Jamaican man. The last time I saw her she was walking up and down Chapel Market with a load of carrier bags and some dirty old coats on her.'

'Spoil they spoil her. I told you that from the time you said how she laughing to herself. I told you is spoil the woman spoil her for her husband,' Uncle Dolphus added.

'You think people would leave their dirtiness behind when they go in other people country,' Miss Alma added.

At that moment the minibus horn sounded around the corner. 'I go call you when I come back Miss Dolphus,' Miss Alma notified her neighbour. 'I'm not staying up there all day.'

'Dolphus, come come. Come and drink the tea,' Aunt Sarh motioned her husband.

'All right woman, all right I coming. You bother me head enough I coming.'

Instead of going back the way he had come Uncle Dolphus walked along the main road and down the steps leading to the verandah. Lappa, the oldest of the three dogs, was lying on the step. It lifted its head, whined, wagged its tail at its master and went back to sleep. Uncle Dolphus took his handkerchief from his pocket, wiped his face, placed the cutlass beside the large tin of mother-in-law's tongue and went inside.

'Sarh oye. Sarh what you going in town today for?' he asked his wife out of curiosity. He went into the kitchen sink, washed his hands and sat down at the table. Aunt Sarh joined him. 'What you going in town for?' he repeated.

'Nothing,' she answered as she poured a cup of tea for her husband and one for herself, out of habit, a habit acquired in England – one never ate without the other.

'How you mean you going in town for nothing,' he enquired.

'I change my mind. I wanted some pressure tablets but I will ask Cherry to buy some for me tomorrow when she go to work.'

'Oh,' Uncle Dolphus sighed. 'Alma niece look well mad. The aunty think is people that put thing on her. Alma believe in too much darkness.'

'Believe! What you mean believe? You don't smell behind the woman's house; eh you don't smell how the place smell like McIntyre doctor's shop. Aaaye. You forget I tell you already that I don't want anything from her to eat. I spend all these years in England snow don't turn me stupidy I'm not coming back home to play careless with my life nuh!' Aunt Sarh exclaimed.

'Ha ha hee hee,' Uncle Dolphus laughed. 'Lord all where you go people believe in darkness. You remember that man that used to walk up and down Upper Street in Islington calling to Lester Piggot and Willie Carson, eh you remember him? Mind you that was different. Was gambling that turned his so, the bookie man that turned him idiot. You remember him nuh?'

'Chupes. How you mean if I remember him? Not the same old stupid man you used to say wanted me? The man looked like that other one who always on the sea wall in Palmiste talking to the fish. I don't know who you take me for. The stupid man up and down the road, sometimes barking like

13

dog and you saying the man after me.' Aunt Sarh was upset, as if at something Uncle Dolphus had said now.

Uncle Dolphus laughed even more. 'He did like you well. Lord; every time you see Joe he walking brisk brisk up and down, up and down Upper Street . . . "go on Lester push him out . . . go on my son go. Look out Willie Carson behind you". The same time he shouting the hand moving like he whipping the horse. Sometimes he would stand for a few minutes, bend over, hold his hands like how the jockey holds the horse's rope when they riding and shout. When he not riding horse he barking like the dogs. Lord this England is a place.'

'I don't know how you could have the nerve to say that man wanted me. You Dolphus sometimes I think you're not right in your head.'

Aunt Sarh was vex but to Uncle Dolphus it was a big joke. 'What about that African man in the black Beetle that used to follow you every evening? He used to wait for you at the top of the road where you lived, you remember?'

That cheered Aunt Sarh up a bit. 'Chupes; you ever see my trouble eh? You ever see my trouble? Aaye the man used to wait for me at the corner of Bromfield Street. There was a time I would go the long way around the other side for him not to see me. In the evenings as soon as I turn round Liverpool Road there was the Beetle parked at the end of Bromfield Street. That African was something else.'

'Go away, you liked the man,' Uncle Dolphus teased. 'You did well like him. If I didn't treat you good by now you would of been somewhere in Africa.'

'Behave yourself. Me? You must be joking. If I liked him I wouldn't even talk to you because he used to follow me long before you said anything to me. The first time I see that big strapping man stepped out of that little car I almost dead

14

with laugh. He looked so funny . . . kunch up kunch up in that little car. In those days the Beetle was the only car Africans used to buy, you remember that? I don't know why they liked that little car so. Some of them could hardly get inside the thing. He used to park in front of the Greek man's house at the end of the street.'

'You was living in that St Lucian man's house I think. I'm not sure if he from St Lucia or Dominica.'

'How you mean you "think", as if you don't know? Ent you and him came friend since you started to come by me? How you mean you think? That man was wicked aye aye. That St Lucian man used to make his wife see trouble. She was such a nice woman, such a nice person. The husband used to treat that Guyanese woman like dirt. She had all those little children and when Friday come you think he coming home with the pay packet? She lucky if she see him till Monday morning. He, his brother and nephew used to go and gamble in a house in Lonsdale Square. Gamble and drink away all the money he work for. Sometimes for the whole weekend Betty don't rest her eyes on her husband. I used to pay her rent but sometimes was me and the Barbadian woman who lived in the top floor room who used to give her little things for those children to eat. Such a nice woman I don't see how she put herself with that old john crow. He was nothing but a old john crow as the Jamaicans would say.'

'He was a bad man; a wicked man in truth. I remember the first evening you let me in your room you had a carrier bag with groceries for them. That was months after I first said anything to you. Lord, girl you gave me a hard time you know, a hard time.' Uncle Dolphus stretched across the table and squeezed his wife's hand. 'You made me walk you know! Lord, woman you made me suffer. First I thought was because

15

of that African man. You told me how he following you, I thought there was something going on'.

'Something going on where! Aaaye the man used to wait for me almost every evening you know. The first time he talked to me he said "I think I know you somewhere". He think he know me somewhere, me, where this African man could ever know me eh where? All of them is the same thing. They always telling woman they know them somewhere. He not only used to wait for me by the road he used to follow me too. Some Fridays when I doing my shopping in Chapel Market every shop I go in when I raise my head was he my eyes meet up on. God that man used to remind me of Idi Amin.'

'You remember the first day he saw us together,' Uncle Dolphus asked as he sipped his tea, 'you remember?'

Aunt Sarh laughed. 'How you mean if I remember? The old head grey but I not dotish yet; how you mean if I remember? Was in the meat shop in the corner of Chapel Market and Penton Street. He had a habit coming in the shop and offering to pay for my meat. Me saye saye. I didn't want anything from that man. The evening he saw you pay for my shopping and then you had to show off by taking the bag in one hand and putting your hand around my shoulder. Lord his face. The man swell up like a bull frog.'

'That was when I was sure of you. The way you turned, said "good evening" in that stuck-up-lady way, and let me hold your hand. I never felt so good since I in England.'

They looked at each other. Their eyes seem to melt into each other, tiny stars twinkling within the brown pupils. Memories flooded. They had had their ups and downs. Theirs was not teenage love. Aunt Sarh left her island in her middle thirties, leaving her two children in the care of relatives. Then the children decided to try to make a life in Canada or

16

America instead of in England with their mother. Neither Aunt Sarh nor Uncle Dolphus had been married before. According to Uncle Dolphus he had never found the right woman. He said he wasn't putting ring on any woman's finger then two days the ring end up in his nose.

Before he met Aunt Sarh he had lived with a woman in Shepherd's Bush, but things had never been good. The woman had had children by another man and she had wanted Uncle Dolphus to mind the children. He said that didn't bother him because if he wanted the woman he expected to look after her children, but the woman was a genal. She used to try to use her brains on him, saying she didn't see the children's father when all the time the man maintaining his children. Not only that but she used always to cry trouble about how she had no money, and what he gave her was never enough. The children didn't have one ounce of manners for him. As soon as he open his mouth to chastise them the first thing they told him was that he was not their father, and the mother encouraging them. Anyway the end came when he found out that all the while he trying to make a life with the woman she had somebody else, had even been buying property in her country with the other man. From that he said he don't trust any woman, but when he saw Aunt Sarh he knew she was special. At first he could not believe that such an upright lady could be by herself, but then he understood why. She was very special.

2

They sat at the table looking at each other. 'Come here girl,' Uncle Dolphus drew back his chair, went over and embraced his wife, burying his face in her cropped hair.

'Behave yourself man. I have work to do,' Aunt Sarh tried to shake off her husband's hand. He held her. She turned her face towards him; brushed her face against his.

'Bow wow wow,' Lappa started barking.

'Who is that? Go and see Dolphus. Go and see who Lappa barking behind.'

'Miss Dolphus, good day, good day maam.'

Uncle Dolphus went to the verandah to meet the caller.

'Aye aye Mr Alvar. Morning morning. I didn't hear you. If the dog didn't bark we wouldn't hear you. Me and the missus inside drinking a cup a tea.'

Miss Dolphus, morning,' Mr Alvar called out to Aunt Sarh as he came on the verandah holding a bag in his hand. 'Miss Dolphus, the wife send a little something for you. They catch a few big jacks this morning but if you not quick you don't even see the scale. When Alleyne catch those little little white cha cha he begging you to take them off his hands, but as soon as is the big jacks they cover them up and head for town as if is only town people mouth that know big jacks.' He

18

handed the bag to Uncle Dolphus, who took it into the kitchen.

Mr Alvar sat down on the bannister. 'You taking a short?' Uncle Dolphus asked. Asking was formality for the answer was always the same. The time of the day was irrelevant when it came to sharing a glass. He went inside, returned with a half bottle of white rum, a jar of water and two glasses.

The sun was cruising its way across the sky. The men charged their glasses. They enjoyed each other's company. Every few minutes someone called greetings to them as they went their way either on foot or from a passing vehicle. Uncle Dolphus enjoyed his Caribbean life. He moved about at his own pace — no more hustling, no more time-keeping. He moved when he wanted to move. Their house was built on a two-acre site. He busied himself cultivating the land around it. He produced provisions for his use and enough to sell to subsidise his pension. His regular customers included the General hospital and some hotels. Along with the provisions he also sold fresh eggs and sometimes milk. The first three years or so he had worked very hard getting the garden into shape. Now he was able to relax and reap the reward. He had kept a few animals, and others he had given to people to care for in return for a share in the animal and any offspring.

Nowadays he hardly went further than the nearest villages. He rarely went to town. He went either to visit special customers or for health reasons. The convenience of either sending his products by special transport or selling to the marketing board truck made things easier for him.

'We hardly see you in Victoria these days,' Mr Alvar said. 'Cousin Mary was saying the other day how you don't even pass by her as you used to. She says perhaps people pounding she name to you.'

Uncle Dolphus laughed, 'Pound she name to me! You

know I don't listen to people. When they want something from you they come with their mouth full of other people's business. I don't have time for that. The missus worse. She always says when she was in England she glad she never lived among too many of our people. To hear how some of these people carry on you will think they on the *Lance* pulling net. They beat combust; beat taybaye. Every week some of them in courthouse. Was a disgrace to see how they have to go and tell these white peole their business. Some of these magistrates and judges don't like black people, but our people will never learn. They think is big they big when they carry on like that.'

'I hear about that courthouse thing you know, Mr Dolphus. I hear about it,' Mr Alvar took a swig at his drink. 'My nephew, that is my sister Christobel's biggest boy, Royston he left his wife for the same thing. He say the woman making confusion with everybody. They used to live in that place you aways talking about – Shepherd's Bush. The way people talking I believe all Grenada people living in Shepherd's Bush. Anyway, my nephew married that woman from up Ducane. Same same way she people love courthouse, down here the same thing she getting on with in England. The last time Royston mother heard from him he moved to Huddersfield. He say as soon as he save up the money he putting in for a divorce. All how his mother write and tell him to try and make his marriage work he say the woman no good. She just like the rest of her family . . . blood thicker than water. I don't know when he will find that kind of money. He always crying trouble. When for him to send something for his mother he crying how England hard.'

'Heh; the place not easy you know Mr Alvar. England! That place is something you know. You really have to tie up if you want anything. When you get the little money in the pay packet on Friday, if you not careful you can't even drink a pint of Guinness. You work like a donkey all week and see what they give you in your hand after they take out a pound for this a pound for that is something else. The most hurtful thing is they giving you all the harder heavier work to do and the white man getting more money than you. If you lucky to see the white man pay packet you shock to see how much more money he get than you. You do all the donkey work and they get the money.'

'Aaye, aye you can't say you not doing the dirty work. If they want you to do it they must pay you. You should tell them, tell them what in you mind,' Mr Alvar commented.

'Tell them! What you talking about? Mr Alvar you don't know these people and them . . . you don't know them at all. As you open your mouth the first thing they tell you is find another job. They sacking you just like that.'

'Is true, true true,' Aunt Sarh joined the men. Whilst drinking Uncle Dolphus and Mr Alvar had started a game of dominoes on the small table kept on the verandah for that purpose. Aunt Sarh didn't play the game but occasionally she would enjoy standing around watching and joining in the conversation. 'Is true,' she continued, 'what you hear Dolphus say is true. These people and them too wicked. They laughing with you good good in your face. Laugh a funny funny kind of laugh like they 'fraid their face will break. The laugh sort of hard – stiff stiff – just jupp and finish. As you turn your back they calling you black bastard. They treat you like rubbish. At first I didn't understand them, when they laughed and make little joke I thought they were all right but bunjay oye I learn about them. I tell you I learn. When I see the way they treat some of us and still laughing is a good thing I believe in God. Is prayers that bring me back home. Prayers, nothing beat back prayers. Once I worked in a laundry in

21

City Road. From Monday to Friday I touting wet towels. Touting wet towels from the washer room to the drying room. Them pushing these big barrow of half-wet towels to the ironing room to iron them. From morning to night working with these wet towels, pushing this heavy barrow. You don't have time to wipe your face. The foreman standing behind you checking to see how many towels you finish pressing. What they used to do was pay you a flat pay and then say you get bonus according to how many towels you finished, that is dry, press and fold up. All week I work work, when Friday come the white women always getting more money than me and the other black woman. I tell you the thing used to hurt me, it used to fret me.

'And Mr Alvar, you working for them. You putting the money in their pocket you think they care anything about you? All they care about is getting their work done,' Aunt Sarh went on. 'There was a St Lucian woman working with me one day she catch her finger in the drying machine . . . slueech the three middle fingers of her left hand gone. Cut out clean clean.'

'She lucky was only she fingers,' Uncle Dolphus added, 'she lucky.'

'You saying that again. Not only that, she lucky was her left hand so she could still use her right hand. The morning that happened one uproar in the place you would think she cut out her fingers by spite. Curse, the foreman started cursing. He cursed even more when he realised that he had to turn off the machine to clean off the blood and had to wash over some of the towels. The poor woman bawling. Her hand pumping blood like when river coming down, and all the man could think about was his work. To take the woman to the hospital was another confusion. In the end she had to wait for the ambulance. All that trouble and was not even the

22

woman's fault. Not her fault at all at all. The man knew
something was wrong with the machine yet he still let people
use it. A man came the week before and told him something
wrong with it.'

'She must get a good piece of money for compensation,'
Mr Alvar commented. 'If was me I putting lawyer on them
same same time. I making them pay. I hear in America when
accident happen they pay out a lot of money. You just put
lawyer on them.'

Mr Alvar had never travelled, not even as far as Trinidad.
Since Uncle Dolphus and Aunt Sarh had returned home he
had become not only a neighbour but a close friend as well.
He was a sort of distant cousin to Uncle Dolphus although
sometimes he said he was related to Mammy and Aunt Sarh
as well. I know that can't be true, because for one thing Uncle
Dolphus didn't belong to the island and Mammy said Mr
Alvar only came to Maran about ten years ago. So I don't
know how he could be related to us. I was only a baby when
Aunt Sarh went to England but like I always known her. She
always wrote to the family, and even after her two children
grew up and went overseas she always knew where her family
was. Not like some people – as soon as they travel it's like
they throw stones behind their backs. I heard Mammy and
Tanty Clarita talking once, well not only once, they always
used to say they didn't know why Sarh left her home to go
to that cold cold place. Aunt Sarh had spent twenty-five years
in England. She only came back once when Mamma died.
She came for the funeral. I remember when she was going
back after the funeral how Mammy cried and cried, telling
her not to go back to England. All the family crying,
telling Aunt Sarh she alone in that cold place. All the close
family at home – if anything happen to her they not around
to look after her. She said she going back only for a couple

23

of years more. Next thing she sent and told us, well not me, but I heard Mammy and them talking, saying Sarh had met up that man and they living together. Was one laugh in the place. Mammy laughed, she laughed, she laughed. You would have thought it was one big joke that Aunt Sarh living with a man.

'Papa, God, world coming to an end?' Tanty June clapped her hands over her head. 'Fancy Sarh living with a man . . . Lord this England must be something oui.' My mother and my aunt laughed like two children when they read that their older sister had decided to live with somebody. Not just anybody, but a man. Lord you should of heard them. According to what I could gather my Aunt Sarh was a very stuck-up person. Nobody was ever good enough for her. When she got pregnant with her two children the family was so shocked at first they thought the children's father hold her down to do what he had to do with her. It was nothing like that though, but she didn't want to marry him. Nobody understood why not. He died in an accident after Aunt Sarh went to England. I heard that my aunt was what you would call poor proud . . . the genuine poor proud. Anyway that was years ago. After she send to say about Uncle Dolphus then he started writing the family and thing. When they got married in England we had a little fete down here for them. All the family came and we enjoyed ourselves.

At first the family was not keen on the man at all. I heard Tanty Clarita and Uncle William talking about how all this time Sarh cutting style on man now she gone quite in England and pick up somebody the family didn't know anything about, although he say he from Grenada. One day Tanty Clarita said she meet up with a cousin of Uncle Dolphus in town. Trust my Tanty Clarita. No matter how dodgy the thing looked, the rest of the family accepted it. They said Aunt Sarh was a

big woman and was she business which man she picked up –
although they worried about her, it was her business. If she
decided to live with him she must know her own mind. As
long as she didn't marry him. Even after she sent to say she
getting married they knew they couldn't do anything, so they
accepted it. It was her business. She was a big woman. That's
what Mammy and the others decided, but not my Aunt
Clarita. She wasn't satisfied. She had to turn detective.
Aunt Sarh and Uncle Dolphus lived together for about four
years before they were married. Was when they decided to
get married that Tanty Clarita really turned detective. To be
honest the whole family was very concerned but was she who
did the investigation. Uncle William said he heard how that
place called England cold and Sarh must want somebody to
keep her warm, especially in the night. All the time they lived
together we did not see one picture of Uncle Dolphus, not
until they married. When the picture came Tanty Clarita find
all kind of fault with the man. The family was a bit worried
because he looked a lot older than her, but we were glad too.

Aunt Sarh never changed. Not like some people, who don't
want to know their family when they travel. She still looked
after us good good. I was her favourite. I think that was
because my mother was her favourite sister. When she sending
things for us I used to get the prettiest dress and there always
used to be an extra ten shillings for 'Dot'. When I was small
she never called me Dorothy, always Dot.

Anyway, as I was saying about Tanty Clarita, as soon as she
heard Aunt Sarh getting married to Uncle Dolphus she get
up hot hot like she had pepper in she skin, saying she must
go and find out who that man's family was in Grenada. The
time she came and say she met a cousin of his in town she
said that she knew who that Dolphus was, but not by that
name. Adolphus Powell was his proper name. His home name

25

was something else. Although he said he from Grenada he really belonged to St Vincent, and St Vincent was just like in Grenada where people always had a home name and a proper name. You get two different names as a baby to prevent jumbie from playing with you. Well, Tanty Clarita found where the family lived in a little village inside River Sallee. She took she farseness and go quite there then come back and say how she didn't like the people who said they were Uncle Dolphus family. He had only one or two relatives there but according to Tanty Clarita these people look as if they didn't wash their hands, and she didn't know what Aunt Sarh want to put sheself with these kind of people for. I think she felt a little better when Aunt Sarh sent to tell us that Unce Dolphus didn't keep in touch with his family. Tanty Clarita said that was a good thing because when he was dead she didn't want his family to come and fight for what he had.

From the letter we knew that Aunt Sarh was very happy with Uncle Dolphus. After a time Mammy and them started calling him 'Brother Dolphus'. He was just like a blood brother. When he and Aunt Sarh retired and came home was like we had always known him. Mr Alvar became like Uncle Dolphus own brother. I think was because all his own brothers were overseas and he and Uncle Dolphus were about the same age that they got on so good. He never travelled. He said he liked to hear all those stories about the big countries, especially England. All of us liked to hear those stories. It was better than taking out tim tim. Some evenings we would sit on the verandah and listen to them. Some of the things Uncle Dolphus and Aunt Sarh had experienced were like story book or watching the theatre. When people go away and write back home they don't tell you everything in the letter. One day Aunt Sarh told us how when she went to England in the early days she felt like she in another world. She said one

26

thing she noticed was that the people didn't laugh at all and when they laugh it never sounded like a laugh. They don't laugh and they don't look at you in the poke of your eyes.

3

'You did feeling good when you go in England Aunt Sarh. Like it better than Grenada?' Desiree asked. She was sitting on the bench in the kitchen shelling some pigeon pease for dinner.

'Feel good! You don't know nothing nuh child. You don't know nothing. The first week I was ready to come back. Ready to pay my passage and come right back to my country.'

'How you mean! If you just reach you had to find out about the place first eh Aunt Sarh? You people didn't come to meet you? They didn't treat you good!'

That Desiree could ask questions. She and Devon, I don't know who could ask more questions. Mammy used to say Devon asked questions worse than Mr Mason.

'Cousin Agnes, that's the person who I went to meet, that woman was something else. Before she went to England she and Mamma moved good good. When she left was Mamma that looked after her two older girls until she sent for them. She was all right then. I think is England that change people so. She sent her husband to meet me at Heathrow airport. First thing she wanted to know when I reach her house was if I had any money to keep me until I find work. She think if I had money I would of left my country eh? Was she encouraged me to come to England. She promised me

28

somewhere to stay until I learn the runnings of the place. If I had sent to tell Mamma how that woman treated me she would of gone mad. Cousin Agnes write and say I mustn't worry she had somewhere for me. Bunjay oye that first night I had to sleep in a little bed with her two young children. A big woman like me had to cooblay on bed with these children; and they rude. Lord these children rude. They didn't know me. First time they rest their eyes on me you should hear the kind of questions they asking me, a big woman. The first night I spend in England I didn't close my eyes. I couldn't sleep. I was very tired but still couldn't sleep. The place was funny funny . . . sort of deady deady. It was in June but I felt like I was in the cemetery on Christmas Eve night.'

'How you mean Aunt Sarh? Christmas time early in the morning the cemetery is kind of cold,' I commented.

'But I thought I hear in June is summer in England,' Desiree said, 'and the sun hot hot like down here.'

'Hot! What hot,' Aunt Sarh grumbled. 'The sun does be hot but nothing like in the Caribbean. I live in that country a long long time and I never felt the sun like real sun. Sometimes the weather does be good when you could walk around without plenty plenty clothes on you. Sometimes I felt like the Syrian only he had his things in his grip on his back. I used to wear mines, that's how it felt anyway. You see the pictures with me wearing the big heavy coat, well sometimes in summer it warm enough that I don't need the coat but that does not last for long. You have to make the most of the few days you get. Only once I remember we had real hot sun. That was in . . . in . . . I think was in 1976. The place hot that water was running out. They started to ration water, saying that people must bathe together.'

'They funny oui. They don't have to tell people to bathe together; we always in the river and sea bathing together.'

29

'Bunjay Christine you stupid oui,' Desiree laughed. 'Is not that kind of bath Aunt Sarh mean. You don't see the big deep basin Miss Avis have in her house. She said that is the bath they have in England. How they think more than one person could go down in this thing and bathe at a time. The people go have to sit on each other and bathe in the dirty water, eh Aunt Sarh? Big place so they don't have enough water. Lord I never hear that yet.'

'Me, I don't think I ever going to stay in these places nuh,' I added. We were busily shelling the pease to cook some rice and pease for dinner. Although Aunt Sarh and Uncle Dolphus did not have children of their own their house was never lonely . . . relations, blood or adopted, church-related relations. Desiree, Devon, Christine, Albert and all the other children who come every day were their unofficial adopted children. Every day after school they come up to help with little work or just come. Not only the children but big people as well always passing or calling out. It's like one family. Many times Aunt Sarh would say that that was one of the things she missed in England. Nobody have time for anybody. If you have a somebody who wants their child to stay with you you had to go to the government people to tell them about it. Aunt Sarh say sometimes the amount of questions they asking you think was passport you buying. I never understand all that.

'So you had to bathe with your neighbour and things like that?' I was a bit curious.

'Neighbour; what neighbour? You don't see neighbour. You could be living in a room in a house for years and you don't know who live in the room next to you. All you hearing is doop doop doop never seeing who making the noise. If you happen to meet up perhaps in front the door they pass you straight straight, not a howdy.'

30

'You didn't hear what Uncle Dolphus did say the last time. You didn't hear he said people even dying in the room next to you and nobody knows dead body in there stinking. Eh you forget when he said that.'

'Hush you mouth Desiree, you lie too much. He didn't say that,' Albert shouted to his cousin.

'Don't tell me to hush my mouth. Ask Uncle Dolphus . . . go on . . . ask him if dead body don't be in the house a long long time stinking.'

'Is that true Aunt Sarh? I never hear that before. Desiree lie too much. She tell too much untruth. Even if some people bad bad they still have friends to call when they passing.'

Aunt Sarh laughed. Not a full full laugh. A sort of side-a-mouth laugh. 'Dolphus, Dolphus you tell those children that?' She aroused Uncle Dolphus where he was sitting on the inside step leading to the downstairs relaxing rooms.

'What you say Sarh? I just sit down here dozing a little. What you say?'

'Is Devon, Albert and Desiree that arguing about something Desiree say you tell her.'

'Uncle Dolphus, ent you say in England that people does dead in their house until they smell bad before other people know they dead? You did say that eh Uncle Dolphus? You did say that. That stupid Albert come saying is untruth I telling.'

Uncle Dolphus climbed two stairs and sat where he could see us. 'Is true true,' he said. 'I know a man died in a house for about three months before they discovered the body. The people that lived next door smell that bad smell they never called health inspector. They kept on using bleach and disinfectant to cover it up. The milk man put milk on the step for about a week then stopped. Even his letter box was blocked up with junk mail. Nobody even wondered what happened

31

to him. Was a council flat he lived in. After a time when the council don't get their rent the housing people went around. They could get no answer when they knock the door. They went for the police to go in with them when they break down the door. When they go inside they find the man dead inside there with his dog.'

'Bunjay his dog an all dead! Lord. You mean people don't pass by him self? Neighbour don't call him in the morning like how you and Miss Alma does call each other?' Devon was puzzled.

'Neighbour,' Aunt Sarh added. 'What neighbour? I tell you that was one thing it took me a long long time to get accustomed to in England. As I does say, you living in a room for years right next door to people and you don't even know their names. When I first went to England I used to try to tell everybody howdy. You know, I used to people saying howdy to each other. I tell you these people used to look at me as if I was mad or something.'

'Chupes,' Desiree sucked her teeth, 'this England is really a funny place boy. A real funny place.'

'Aye aye child you think you know anything.' Aunt Sarh continued. 'You think you know anything. I tell you you saying howdy they looking at you as if you come from another planet. Could be why so many black people in the mental hospital. The doctors don't understand us. The people don't understand. They not even making the effort to understand us. If we laugh loud, they say is mad, we mad. We raise we hand when we talking, they say is attack, we attacking them. They have a thing, I think even now, well I hear it worst now, they call us schizophrenic. Any little thing doctor write that the person suffering from schizophrenia.'

'Skip so what?' Desiree asked.

'Yes, that is what they saying black people suffering from.

32

That is what they calling us now. They saying we like two people in one. We change from one to the other quick quick.'

'They mean we mad then, eh that's what they saying. As soon as a black person say anything is mad they mad.' My head was shaking like how the pease dropping in the bowl.

'Dorothy, I tell you, you don't know nothing. When these people and them going to school to study for all these kind of jobs they should have black people to train them as well. Then they would understand us. I glad I not in that place but I sorry for some of us up there especially the older ones. I see with my two eyes what they could do to you especially if you don't have anybody that could stand up and speak up for you. You have little problem, you go to them for help because you paying your National Insurance for things like that, when you think is help they helping you they making matters worse. You go to doctor, before you push your head in the door he start writing prescription. Sometimes you go for headache when you catch yourself they give you pills for bad foot. Some of them don't have time to listen to you. All the doctors do is feed you on drugs. In the end sometimes you end up in the mental hospital and you are not mad.'

Aunt Sarh was getting upset as she related these stories to us. She was busy busy cooking the breakfast but you could see she was upset.

'You remember that Dominican woman that was working in the Royal Free Hospital with your friend Miss Lynette, Sarh?' Uncle Dolphus recalled. 'You remember how they picked up the woman and threw her in the mental hospital in Leytonstone saying she was a mental case when nothing was wrong with the woman?'

'Aaaye, you ever see trouble so,' Aunt Sarh picked up the story. 'You ever see that. The woman had a bit of family problem. I think at the time on top of what problems she had in England her brother died in Dominica in accident so obviously the body felt run down. She said she wasn't sleeping, and she worried because she couldn't find the money to go to be with her family in Dominica. She went to her panel doctor for something to help her to sleep. I think she more wanted somebody else to talk to apart from the people she knew. Anyway, while she was at the doctor surgery she and this white woman catch up. In her vexation she started to speak the patois. Speaking the patois and waving her hand about. I don't know how they managed it but between the receptionist and the doctor they got ambulance to come and take the poor woman to the Claybury mental hospital. Push needle of drugs in her skin and take her to hospital. When her family looking for her to come home next thing they got phone call telling them she had nervous breakdown and she in hospital under section this that and the other. Just just so they turned the woman into a mental case. All how she telling them they wrong they saying they know what was best for her. I hear when she in the hospital she started praying. She telling them nothing wrong with her they won't hear so she started calling on the Lord for deliverance. Well was then they pushed drugs in her skin saying they had to calm her down because she had thing in her head. When she called on the Lord Jesus one nurse shouted at her to shut her mouth she don't know what she saying.'

'Aunt Sarh you mean these people don't know about Jesus Christ? They don't know how to pray? What happened to the woman? She must get mad after they treated her like that,' Marie added.

'Well was a good thing she had family who know how to handle those people. When they telling you they know what is best for you you must know how to handle them to make them see you know better. But she had to stay in that hospital

34

a few weeks before they managed to get her out you know. A good few weeks. A good good few weeks.' Aunt Sarh's voice kind of drifted away.

'I tell you some of these doctors have something to answer for. You go to them they not even sounding you before they write out pills for you to take. A good thing I didn't used to bother with them much. You trying to tell them what wrong they not listening. Give you wrong drug then say they sorry. They don't listen sometimes, saying they don't understand. How they go understand when they don't listen eh how?' Uncle Dolphus was more vexed than Aunt Sarh.

'Everytime they don't understand what we saying they say we schizophrenic,' he continued. 'The thing is, some of them don't know the real meaning of the word at all. Those that know what it really means don't care about the people that suffering anyway. They quick quick to say is split person- ality. Quick quick to say the person is violent when sometimes is nothing so. Nothing so at all at all. When they find someone who really suffering from the illness they just chuck them aside. Chuck them aside and pump them up with all kind of drugs. When the body get used to one set of drugs they pump a stronger one. All that time the body getting weaker and weaker. Sometimes some drug might work but the doctors don't find out exactly how far the person gone in the first place. Not just doctor that don't understand. Not just the doctors at all.'

'Could be why the neighbours don't say howdy, Aunt Sarh. Could be because they don't understand you eh? Perhaps was that.' Devon added his own verdict. Like everyone he loved to listen to stories from Aunt Sarh and Uncle Dolphus. I tell you some of these stories make you feel like you want to fight and cuss bad word. Imagine turning the poor woman into drug addict . . . aaaye . . . Turn her into drug addict you know.

35

That's what will happen if they keep pushing needle in the skin. You ever hear thing so . . . eh.

'Heem cooum cooum,' Aunt Sarh cleared her throat. Sometimes as if she and Uncle Dolphus take turn to tell the stories. 'Is so they doing all the time all the time,' she began. 'There was another time they wanted to take this woman children from her. They started saying she suffering from some kind of mental disorder. Not a thing wrong with the woman. Nothing wrong with the husband or the family. Nothing. They didn't even go to welfare for help. Nothing. What happened was the health visitor went to the house to check on the baby. When she got there the two older children were in a room playing quietly. One had four and the other two and a half. The children playing while the baby sleeping. The health visitor asked the mother how the children so quiet. She never see children so young so quiet. The mother laughed. She told her they only quiet for a few minutes as they just had their bath and meal and she trying to prepare lunch for when her husband come. The health visitor sat down in the kitchen playing friendly friendly. What the woman didn't know, didn't realise, was that the other one was taking notes. While she pretending to be interested in the children was notes she taking to go and make report. While the mother picking the rice to cook the health visitor watching her. Aye aye next thing you hear was social worker knocking on the people door saying they come to take the children away for their own benefit. You should hear the nasty report the health visitor made on that woman. You should hear it. She said although the children seemed healthy and happy something must be wrong with them because she never see young children like that so quiet, and what concerned her most was that the mother sit down at the kitchen table counting rice grain. Checking out the black grains, then the white

36

in a basin. She said the mother must be mentally disturbed to act in that way. For that reason she recommend the children be taken into care for their own safety. Well they didn't bargain for the children father.'

'Miss Dolphus you joking. You mean these people don't know you have to clean the rice before you put it in pot?'

'Aaaye Miss Alma you dey. I didn't hear you self.'

'I did hear she call cousin Dorothy, she call when Uncle Dolphus quarrelling about how England doctor don't listen to people.' Devon informed us.

'I didn't want to disturb you all so I just sit down here. But Miss Dolphus these people and them they don't good. What they mean something wrong with you if you cleaning rice before you put it in pot eh . . . bunjay oye. The more I live the more I hear.'

'Saye saye you think it easy in England. Miss Alma you think it easy? Because these people live one way they don't try to understand other people at all.'

'Could be why they neighbours don't say howdy. Perhaps they don't understand what you saying. Perhaps was that, eh Aunt Sarh,' Devon repeated.

'Hypocrite, they hypocrite. They playing them don't understand you but everything you do in your room they know to bring news on you. You living in number fifteen, you don't know who living in number sixteen, but number seventeen know your business more than you. They had a habit peeping behind the curtain. You don't see any face all you noticed is the curtain kind of blowing. Sometimes they quiet quiet in their room make you think they not in all the time is listening they listening to your business. A thing they used to do was to put a glass against the wall and press their ears on the glass to hear what you saying next door,' Uncle Dolphus added.

37

'Bunjay; these people and them farse oui. I didn't know white people so farse.' Desiree was astonished.

'Aye aye, what do this child at all. Anybody farse more than white people. They don't say farse like us, they say nosey. Quick quick to call each other "nosey parker".' Everybody laughed when Aunt Sarh said that. 'Still was not all of them so, you find some nice people in England but I don't trust them at all. I always watched my tongue with them.'

'Sarh you don't finish cooking yet. The worms in my belly bawling.'

'Aaye how come you hungry already not just now dey you drink tea? Eat a piece of cake and drink a glass of juice, the breakfast soon ready.' Aunt Sarh turned towards the stove and started stirring the callaloo.

She said she was going to cook rice and pease then she changed her mind. She decided to do callalloo instead. She offered Miss Alma the pease. No matter what we doing stories about England always come out. One little word put the memory in motion. At first I think they missed the country more than they were admitting but as time passed by they were happy telling of the things that had happened to them there, kind of reliving the tales naturally.

4

When I am working I go up to their house every evening. I like keeping Aunt Sarh company a bit although she is not lonely. Sometimes we sit under the house, outside under the trees or like Uncle Dolphus and Mr Alvar, sitting down on the verandah. Sometimes they tell a story from beginning to end, other times it is as though they forget to tell us something, when they remember they must finish the story. Especially Aunt Sarh, like she forget something she was saying yesterday and when remembers she must tell the story. Sometimes I think she brains going because at time she mix up one thing with another and she and Uncle Dolphus start a confusion because he say is not so. They don't really vex though. We all just laugh when she come out with 'the one little piece of brain cell I have going'. That's really funny. Not her brains going, but how she come out with things. She is like that, start one thing then forget about it and talk about something else then say something referring to what we were saying before — sometimes not a long dialogue just one sentence and on to something else. Like the time she told us about neighbours in England. We finish talking about that long long. Everybody forget about England and England neighbour. We talking about how the new priest in the Anglican church changing up everything. As soon he come he want to change the service. Everybody accustom to seven o'clock mass every second and fourth Sunday in the month and nine o'clock on the other Sundays, but he talking about mass five o'clock in the morning. Soon as he come breeze don't pass but he start changing things. The man must be crazy or something – I don't know who he expect to leave their house to get to church five o'clock in the morning. Not so much leaving your house, but the piece of road you have to walk not good especially around All Saints' time. People say they meet up all sort of devil in the road doing their nastiness. Anyway, that's what we were talking about sitting downstairs chipping coconut to make coconut sugarcake when all of a sudden Aunt Sarh burst out with 'I don't bother with them at all at all.'

'Who?' I asked.

'How you mean who? Those English people nuh. I didn't used to bother with them at all. I just used to go about my business.'

Then she laughed. Laughed one of her little side-face laughs.

'One thing I used to like was Sunday market.'

'Sunday Market? People don't go to market on Sunday! What's about church?' I was surprised.

'Chil, to tell you the truth I shame to tell people when I first went to England I didn't go to church. When I left my country I was a pillar in the church. A pillar. Everything in church is me. Sunday school, choir, Mother's Union, everything, Sarah Blackburn was there. I made up my mind to follow up my church when I went to England. The first time I put my foot in the church, was about a month after I landed in the country. I tell you the Sunday morning I put on my clothes, take up my hymn book with my Bible, say I going to church. I tell you something if anybody tell you they see

40

the devil face to face believe them. Lord, when I in that church I couldn't see God at all. I mean God wasn't in the church at all at all.'

'Perhaps you were looking for your regular black God,' teased Uncle Dolphus. 'These people and them think God is white. You ever see a picture of a black God! According to them Jesus white. The blessed Virgin Mary white, you don't expect God to be black do you?'

'Chupes. Dolphus you always with your stupidness. God is just God. Stupid people that putting colour into everything dividing up people. Mind you I saw a picture of a black Virgin Mary with a black Jesus in a Church of England in Leytonstone, you know. Mind you, if you really think about it the part of the world where Jesus was born and the way you read about his hair and things he couldn't be white. To me God is God. I never used to look at his colour, but in England everything is to do with colour. These people make the colour of your skin a problem. When I growing up in Grenada people was just people. There was rich people and poor people. Some white people but they were just people. Everybody went to church to worship one God. In England, ehh, that place is something. As I was saying, God wasn't in the church that morning at all. Every time I look up on the altar was the devil standing in front of me. Every time I try to pray everything just mix up in my head. And the people they so cold. I don't mean because it might be winter, I mean there was no warmth in there to encourage you. They treated you like you intruding. I couldn't wait for the service to be over to get out of that place. Was a long long time before I put my foot back inside a church again. Everyday I read my Bible and say my prayers. You need to believe strongly in God to survive. I don't think you bound to raise a heavy Bible under your arm every Sunday to go to church to believe

41

in God. God is everywhere. He hears you wherever you are. Every morning everynight I go down on my knees and talk to God. I said I'm not putting my foot back in the church because I can't talk to God there.'

'So instead of going to church on Sunday you used to go to market!' I was inquisitive.

'What you saying Dot? Sarh loved a street market. Your Aunt loved a Sunday market,' Uncle Dolphus added.

'Yes man . . . aye, aye, what do you. Sundays you get all kind of bargains. Things like clothes and wares you getting cheap cheap. Not only clothes to put on you but bedspread and pillowcases, everything. All those nice candlewick bedspread you see I have, in Chapel Street market I bought most of them. There was this man who used to sell plates and cups and things like that. Lord, I don't know how he used to do it. He would spread cups, plates and saucers on a big piece of cloth on the ground, climb on a stool and juggled plates on his arms . . . four or five at a time. He threw them in the air and catch them. Was like in a circus. I never see him break one plate. He used to sell his wares real cheap. All those nice pretty plates with the cups and saucers in the cabinet inside, was from him I bought them. Years, years now you know. This man used to sell those big dinner plates for ten shillings; that was before they changed the English money. I had this Jamaican friend called Queenie. We used to go to the market practically every Sunday. We used to throw sou sou together and when we get our hand would buy things to send back home. I had two big trunkful of things. One thing that woman red eye, she red eye. Everything that I buy she wanted me to get one for her and if I don't ask her for the money I never get a cent. Both of us working for the same money but I must spend mines on her. I tell you these Jamaicans is something else. We used to throw the sou sou, the woman would get

42

her hand and save up all her money and turn around and ask me to lend her money to send her children to school. Those children father was living in New Cross, but he used to maintain his children. She self tell me how much money he used to give her for the children. You think she'll spend the money on the children? She! Not a penny. You should see the state of those children. The old shabby coat she used to send the girls to school in. All the woman did was put her money in the bank saying she saving to go back to Jamaica to open business. Hide all her money and turn around and borrow from people. When she borrow she don't want to pay back. She was the most bad pay person I ever come across in my life. She had a thing she used to say that if she spend her own money it finish but if she borrow she had to pay back. After a time I stop lending her my money. Aye aye after all my mother didn't christen me damn fool. She thought she had brains. Had a way they calling us small island. When I catch up on the way she operated I tell you kur-kurt eat she name.

We used to go to all different Sunday markets not only Chapel Market. We would go all the way down East Street to get nice net curtains. Then sometimes we went to Petticoat Lane. Lord that England is something yes. Big big Sunday people dress up when you think was church they going. Chupes; which church. Some of these people don't know God. Some of them their God is the pub, that's the rum shop, true true. When you see them well dressed up is down the market or in the pub they going. When I first heard about market opening on Sundays I thought was people passing around with their suitcases selling things like the Syrians and them used to do in Grenada. But saye saye big big market. You getting every every thing. And so people thiefing your things. You in the crowd you have to hold on to your purse tight tight because before you blinked your eyes your money gone.

'The first Sunday market I went to was Chapel Street. I was living in Lonsdale Square at the time. One weekend my cousin in Wembley came to spend time with me. Since the Friday night she came she on about how she hear about a Petticoat Lane market. You hear Dolphus saying how I love Sunday market, my cousin Muriel worse. She is what I call a Sunday market fanatic. Anyway, we went down the Lane the Sunday morning. I was shocked. I never see a market so big. It take up a whole whole road and all the side roads as well. If you put the road stand up sort of straight to the sky it'll be like a tree with branches spread out. Each branch is a market itself but still part of the big market. Every part full up full up of all different kind of things. And people! Lord! You see all kind of people in that place some of them not buying anything only looking for trouble. Was the first time I saw people walking the street covered in black from head to foot, like that old woman on the *Lance*. They cover up even their noses. The only part of the body you could see was the little slit for the eyes. Over the nose was a kind of veil to let them breathe. It's all part of their religion and things like that. They don't trouble people. They just move about in their own world.

'Another Sunday I went to Petticoat Lane by myself. I saw this stall with these pretty dresses. There was this one in particular that I liked. I went to buy for Dorothy and one for another little girl. The one on the rack was the right size for one so I asked the woman if she had a bigger size. She looked at me as if I was mad. I said I wanted the one on the rack and a bigger one. The white woman turned her back on me saying I am a stupid black bastard. Aye aye just so the woman insulted me. I told her she was the stupid ignorant

44

one, she don't have to be so rude. Was then I really had the shock of my life. A black woman standing in front me had her hand full of clothes. She turned around and told me that was one of each dress there was because it was secondhand clothes. I didn't understand. Couldn't see why that had to make the other woman so rude. When she said secondhand I thought it was from the factory and something was wrong with it. Because the woman who lived in the back room to me in Canonbury Square used to work for a factory sewing at home. When there was clothes that wasn't stitched straight or anything like that Mr Levley would sell them to her for half price or even cheaper and she used to sell them. I thought that was secondhand but when the black woman went on to tell me that it was clothes other people wear and they don't want well I couldn't believe it. And the woman had her hands full of people old clothes to send to her people back home. Me! I could never put people old clothes on my back, and I definitely would not buy them to send to anybody I know. The woman so proud she started telling me that those clothes are good because some of them is from people that died without wearing them. When she said that my blood walked all over my body. I couldn't help it; my face change. I just turned my back and walked away. You should hear the long chupes she let out behind me.

'People could really make themselves worse than they are. If I could buy one dress I buy one new dress, not two and three and is other people rubbish. Not me at all all.'

I laughed. Not at what Aunt Sarh said but the way she said it. Sometimes she get herself well vex, real vex you know. I could just picture her face when she cut eyes at that woman . . . and the mouth. When she skin that mouth you think is scorn she scorning you; I could just imagine her face

45

that morning. She never shout or quarrel with anybody but the look she look at you alone is enough.

5

I came up early that morning to do the washing because I had to go out. Aunt Sarh asked me to chip some coconut for her to make sugarcake while Devon and Desiree grate some to make a bottle of oil.

'Miss Dolphuuus, Miss Dolphus oye rain coming, rain coming. Yu clothes wetting.'

Was a good thing Miss Alma called because we didn't have rain to study. The sun splitting earth. No rain set up. The clothes dry already. If Miss Alma didn't call they would wet up.

'Aye aye that rain funny oui,' Uncle Dolphus said, scanning his eyes over the sea. 'It not falling in the sea at all. This rain falling just like London rain.'

'Chupes. What you talking about London rain. In that place you don't see rain set up. It just fall straight straight from the sky. Sometimes it make a little dark like the sun cover its face. Just a little because the place always grey grey.' Aunt Sarh sluish her hand across her eyes as if wiping away the greyness. 'Sometimes only when you look outside and see the ground wet you know rain fall.'

'You don't hear it falling on the galvanise?' asked Devon.

'Hear what on the galvanise? You don't hear nothing. The houses in England don't have galvanise like our houses, they

47

don't even have nail. When rain falling the only time you might hear anything is if hailstone falling knocking the window boaw boaw doaw like people stoning you inside the house. If you outside the grains burning your face like salt.'

'The rain falling just like the snow,' Uncle Dolphus added, like an afterthought.

'Snow,' Devon repeated. 'I'll like to see snow boy. I hear it like shave ice. If I in London I'll eat it for so.'

'Lord this thing fall on my head oui. My head take this snow you know. Almost thirty years this thing fall on my head . . . almost thirty years. The thing falling on you and you hardly feel anything. When I burning bush and the bits flying I call it snowflake in the sun. It look just like the snow . . . just like snowflake.'

Uncle Dolphus left the stairs and sat at the dining table. Miss Alma came inside the house, the pot of callaloo soup merrily whispering on the stove. Aunt Sarh brought out a bottle of ginger beer, glasses and a plate of coconut tart. She invited Uncle Dolphus and Miss Alma to help themselves and poured some drinks into cups for the children.

'Dorothy, help yourself you know. I know you funny. Funny just like your mother. If I don't call your name you not touching nothing. Anyway, not only you and your mother it run in the family. We don't let people make us shame. Nobody insulting us for their things. I rather go without before I let anybody make me shame.'

Uncle Dolphus took a mouthful of ginger beer, 'Sarh it don't have ice in the icebox, bring a piece nuh. The ginger beer strong like any liquor.' He rolled the glass between the palms of his hand. Eyes staring out the window through the leaves of the coconut trees. At the bottom of the house the rain had hardly fallen, everything was dry. The sun had outwitted the rain. The leaves were quite still as if in obedience to the sun's command. The old man's eyes glided along the sea bed. It seemed as if his thought were meandering like the tiny waves as they bobbed about.

'Snow,' he murmured to himself, 'snow.' He wiped his hands across his face as if brushing away the snowflakes. 'Hmmm, I remember the first time I saw snow. The first first time I saw these bits of white things flying about like bits of cotton wool in the sky. I was working in a glass factory in Wembley. That's another thing you know, another thing. Was the second job I had in the country. I stayed there for about ten years. I worked in another factory before I went there. Those days there was the labour exchange where they try to find you work. Just before we left the country all that changed . . . everything changing. Sometimes I don't know why they changing because some things worse than before. Anyway, the man from the labour exchange sent me to that place. He told me they looking for someone who is hardworking, not lazy and would not go off sick every day because they were always busy. I could learn about furniture making and on top of that the money was good. He asked me if I wanted to give it a try. I said yes. After all, I didn't leave my country to come and sit down in another man country. Is work I came to work. I had it all planned out. I was going to spend five years and go back home and start up my business again. Open my little rum shop, put somebody in it during the day while I plant my cultivation and look after some animals and things like that. And was true. I told the man I didn't mind hard work at all. He rolled his tongue, went on about how was a younger person they looking for but if I think I could manage he will send me for the interview. I don't know what stupidness that man was talking. I was a young man in my prime. Only in my thirties. Anyway, he phoned the place and set up an interview. I tell you these people and them have good good curse. God turn his back on some of them you know. When the man telling me all these things I thinking was true and planning things in my head. Thinking how I was lucky to find a job just two weeks in the country. I thinking that I would soon catch up on the runnings and start saving to go back home to set myself up. When he said furniture factory I even thought perhaps I could learn how to make those nice nice chairs and things I see in the stores and do something like than when I went back. It would be a change of plan but perhaps better. Anyway, he gave me the address and even told me which buses to catch to get to the place. When the man at the gate saw me the first thing he opened his mouth and say was we don't have any vacancy. When I showed him the paper the man from the labour exchange gave me he turned it up and down about three times then asked me my name about three times, before he called somebody inside to tell them I was there. A man came from inside a little room on the side like and I saw both of them watching me on the side of their eyes. They talking and watching me on the sly. I sat down on a little bench where the gate man told me to sit and waited.'

'They gave you the job though Uncle Dolphus. They did give you the work?' Nigel asked, that's Miss Nellie's grandson, Miss Nellie from over the road by the big golden apple. He often come to meet Devon and like the others make Uncle Dolphus home his home. 'They did give you work because you could do all the things the man said they was looking for eh!'

'True I could do all those thing, but hear. A few minutes afterwards the first man came back to me with one of those plastic smiles on his face. I thought well he smiling with me he must like me and will give me the work. "Hey Johnny," he

50

said. All black man was Johnny to them. "Hey Johnny if we take you on when can you start?" Just like that. I felt good. I said I could start straight away or perhaps tomorrow; that would of been the Thursday. He said he would preferred if I started the next Tuesday because that was the beginning of their week. That was another thing, their working week start anytime they want. He asked me for my P45. I told him I only just come into the country. He said never mind they would sort out everything. We arranged for me to start work on Tuesday.

'I remember it clear as if it was last week. It was Tuesday the 22nd of September. I couldn't wait. My cousin Dora made me some sandwich and a flask of tea. She was one good woman . . . a good good woman. She and her husband looked after me when I first landed in England. They always say that good people don't last long. Boysie was like my own flesh and blood. Was he first showed me how to get around London. Mind you it didn't take me long to find my way around. As long as I had an address and the bus fare I was all right.'

Aunt Sarh had started dishing out the food. The strong sweet callaloo soup hit the nose like a thunder bolt. 'The food ready but all you have to wait for it to cool a bit,' she made a general announcement.

'You didn't loose you way that Tuesday, did you Uncle Dolphus?' I teased.

'What you mean loose his way? You could see Mr Dolphus losing his way anyway,' Miss Alma said.

'That Tuesday morning I got up bright and early. Bright and early ready to start work,' Uncle Dolphus continued. 'Take up the things Dora made for me and off to work thinking I will be learning to make fancy furnitures. Aaye aaye, saye saye first when I reached to the gate the man didn't

51

want to let me in. He was not the same one who was there when I went there first. All I trying to tell the man I starting work he won't listen. I told him my name and everything. He had to phone the office before he would let me in. I don't know why but from that time I was planning for him. There was something in the way he talked to me that I didn't like at all. When I went in the man who took me on came into the yard to meet me with the same plastic smile on his face only this time I noticed he was not looking at me in my face. His eyes and mines not making two at all. He told me to follow him. He went through some dirty dirty corners until he reached a kind of box room where they stored brooms and brushes and cleaning things. The man turned to me and tell me to look inside I will find an overall to put on to protect my clothes. Although I saw it was a cleaner's cupboard I still wasn't thinking that way. I still thinking because they making furniture the place will be dusty and the overall was to keep my clothes clean. All that time I didn't ask the man about my pay. I thought I'll start the job first, see how it went then negotiate pay. When I told Boysie that in the evening he told me when they offered me the job the first thing I should do was to ask about the money. You learn day by day. Anyway, the man asked me if I mind sweeping up the yard outside for him. I asked him what he mean. He said the person who usually sweep up was off sick so if I don't mind just cleaning up for them. I didn't like that all but I agreed to do it still thinking things will get better. He showed all where he wanted me to sweep. By then I really started thinking. He must of looked at me as some kind of idiot. I asked him when would I start working in the factory as the man in the labour exchange said. Was then he told me that the job they sent me for was already gone. He went on to say that he didn't know that when he spoke to me last week. "What you mean gone? If the job gone what am I doing here?" I asked. He said they expected to have another vacancy in a few days and they think I will fit in, that's why they decided to keep me on. If I don't mind cleaning that is only temporary. I then asked him about the pay. He said not to worry the pay will be all right. I didn't like that but decided to watch and see. That first day I sweep. I never seen a place so dirty in my life, to see was a place people moving every day. That evening going home I got talking to a black man going through the gate. We brango a bit. He said he was glad to see another black face in that place because he does feel out of place as the only black person in the whole big place. He asked me what I was doing. When I told him his face changed. He opened his mouth to say something and stopped. By that time we reached the gate he went one way I went another. Next morning I turned up for work early eager to find out if anything new about a proper job. The foreman called out to me before I even clocked my card.

' "Hey Johnny," he said, "You did a good job yesterday. I am really pleased with you." My mind starting running. What on earth this man talking I do a good job? The man gave me a broom to sweep and he come praising me. What is this at all aaaye.

' "I wonder if you could start over here," ' he pointed to the other side of the yard.

'I started to feel bad. Not sick but bad. I looked at the man, his face like inside a fish gill. I looked at him my mouth half opened. I felt the cold going through my teeth. Although was only September I was feeling the cold already. When I said I cold they laughed at me saying wait until November when the cold really start. According to the English September is still in summer. I always thought summer was when it make hot. I tell you something I was learning fast. Learning everything fast. Anyway I followed the foreman around the corner.

' "I want you to start cleaning up here like you did yesterday. Sweep up here. There is bucket and mop in the cupboard for you to use to wash down the toilet." '

'I looked at him, "Me!" I said. I just couldn't believe it. I went for a job making furniture.

' "What's wrong?" he asked. "You understand what I say don't you?"

'That was adding insult to injury. "You want me to clean the latrine?" I asked, sure and still not sure that was what I heard. That time I tell you the piss in the toilet kicking bucket. That man stood in front me bold bold and tell me that is the only job he had for me. If I don't want it I know what I can do. I looked at him plump in his face "Kiss my ass," I said. "Kiss my ass. I didn't leave my country to come here to clean white man piss and shit. You kiss my ass." I didn't even look behind me or looked left or right. I picked up my bag and walked straight of the gate.

'Just imagine, first job in England that man giving me broom and bucket telling me to wash and clean latrine. Me! I hear people went to England because they that badly off in their own country. I sorry for them. I wasn't that badly off to jump in to clean white man shit. I just tell the man to kiss my ass . . .'

We started laughing. Desiree shouted out 'Bunjay oye!'

'Dolphus man mind you mouth. Mind you mouth man children in front of you,' Aunt Sarh rebuked him. 'Is a long long time that happened man, forget that.'

'I know it's long time but still I don't forget. These people looked on us as some kind of beast. Like we don't have any feelings.' The old man groaned as if remembering pained him.

'Did you go back to the labour place and tell them what

54

happened eh Uncle Dolphus? What happened? Did they send you back there or something?' Devon always asking more questions than everybody else.

'Devon boy you have to stand up for yourself. Stand up for yourself otherwise they walk all over you. And they all stick together. The evening when I told Cousin Dora what happened Boysie said I should cuff down the man for his farseness. They take black people for rubbish. Boysie got me two days work with a mate of his. He wanted me to apply for a job where he worked on with London Transport but I didn't like that kind of work. The kind of hours they had to work was not to my liking. At the time the Post Office used to always take on people. I thought of applying but couldn't make up my mind. You had to take medical exam for these jobs and I didn't like the sound of that. Not that there was anything wrong with me, I just didn't feel happy about taking medical exam to get a job. Anyway, I stayed with Boysie mate until about the end of November when I got another job. A proper job. Was a big firm making glass. These people and them clever boy. On one side they making the plain glass then other part of the factory they turning it into different shapes and style. That was where I was working when I saw snow for the first time. I was there for about two weeks when the water freeze up. They explained to me how it happen and if they don't get it thaw out the pipes will burst. I tell you that time I walking about like the Syrian clothes shop . . . a vest, three pullover, one jacket and a heavy coat on my back. I bought a big heavy winter boots. My foot felt tired just putting them on. With all that I still cold. The clothes on me felt like a bundle of wood how they heavy. I walking about with my hands deep deep in my pocket. Anyway one evening I heard them talking about how the temperature rise enough for it to snow. That was puzzling because I thought that it was the cold that made the snow or something like that. They said when the snow fall it will get a little warmer.'

'The more I hear about this England the more it make me wonder. I will like to go there for the experience, but I don't think I will ever live there,' commented Miss Alma.

'The place funny just like the people. Just like the people. One minute they laughing with you next they turn. The people funny funny,' Aunt Sarh added.

'Emmm,' Uncle Dolphus grunted. 'When I heard that I started praying for the snow to fall. Anything to make me feel warmer. I wanted to take off some of the clothes on my back. Even in bed you have to cover under how many blanket, wear a whole load of clothes in bed. Worse when you alone in that bed. That's why I pick up with that woman in Shepherd's Bush. I couldn't stand another winter in a cold bed.'

'Eh, em,' Aunt Sarh cleared her throat at the same time cutting her eyes at her husband.

'That night even Boysie and Cousin Dora talked about how by morning snow will be on the ground. Next morning I woke up looking for the snow – nothing. All I saw was the ground wet wet and kind of shining. As soon as I put my foot in front the door I slipped. Was a good thing the boots had grips. On my way to work these bits of things started flying about. Flying about like pieces of rain. Not raindrops but pieces of rain. I met one of my work mates at the bus stop, his head covered, his hands deep down in his pocket. You could only see the blue eyes grinning. "Hi Adolphus," he said, "how goes it this morning? Did you see the snow last night? It really came down. I thought that it would settle but rain came with it and washed it away."

'He was talking to me but not really expecting an answer. I was praying for the bus to come. This bits of flying things were coming stronger. My feet felt like two thick pieces of frozen ice only heavier.

' "We in for some heavy falls by the weekend," Dermot informed me as we climbed the bus. As we sat down he looked at me as if seeing me for the first time. "Hey Adolphus this is the first time you see snow isn't it? You people must be totally bonkers to leave your warm country to come here." I wanted to say something but the last thing I wanted to be reminded about at that moment was the Caribbean. I was feeling homesick enough without more reminders.

'Once we inside the factory we don't see outside until we finished in the evening. Lord, I was in for a shock. When I looking for ground I see this white carpet in front me. Everywhere covered in white. I hesitated. Jesus Christ, I thought, how am I going to walk in this thing? I looking at the people leaving. Chup chup chup this thing crunching under their feet. Lord how am I going to walk in this thing? "Come on Dolphus, man this is it" Wesley patted me on the back. "You can't sleep here man." Everybody turned up their collar, some covered their heads, hands deep in pocket and headed out. I followed. Chup chup chuup the snow crunching under people feet. Many times I slipped before I reached where I was living. The thing that made it worse was that early early it started to get dark. Since about three o'clock night started coming down.'

'You mean the moon shining since in the evening?' Cynthia asked.

'Moon, you don't see moon in England. Especially in winter. The sky just dull and grey all the time.' Aunt Sarh volunteered the information. 'You don't see moon and if you see the sun it kind of far far away, dull dull without any warmth at all. Sometimes the sun look as if it tired.'

'Warmth! In the winter the more the sun shine the colder

57

it is,' Uncle Dolphus continued. 'Heh all how I tried to be careful I still ended on the ground. Was the next morning the ground bad, it bad. The snow had stopped falling. The sun was shining. Shining a kind of sharp sharp brightness like when you flashing glass at the sun itself. Chup Chup sloup sloush everybody trying to make their way to wherever they were going. I managed to reached the factory gate all right. Just as I turned to go inside the door my foot slipped as when you slip on mango skin in the rain season. Sleesh sleesph I went down plamp on my bam. The more I tried to get up the more I slide down. People just hustling inside. Was the same Wesley that gave me a hand to reach inside. I shame. I shame. Big man like me on the ground like a little child. But nobody laugh or anything like that. That was the first fall. God knows how many more I had before I left England. One thing though, the firm was not bad to work for at all. When the snow bad and you can't get in they would see with you, even let you go home early when the weather bad. Some other firms look to give you the sack if you late. You couldn't open your mouth and say you late because of bad weather. They give you your card quick quick. Mind you, you had to work you know. You had to work. The foreman used to say you give him value and he will treat you all right. I remember him good good. He was from New Zealand . . . Steve something or the other.'

'Perhaps because he was not English why he was nice, eh Uncle Dolphus? Perhaps.'

'I don't think so, Desiree. He wasn't English but he was white. Not all the white people was that bad. Not that they liked black people but some of them treated us like people.'

Aunt Sarh laughed. Not her hearty hearty laugh. 'Not all of them bad. If you meet up a nice one they treat you like people. But the others they go on as if when they eat is not the same mess they mess like black people. They laugh with you a kind of smile, just "zoop" across the lip and that's it. They don't laugh like us. Deep down in the belly laugh. Real hearty happy laugh. Only one little "zoop" and they finish. And they don't look at you in the eye you know. When you working with them they give that "zoop" laugh you thinking is friendly they friendly, just wait until something happen. Like the time the machine cut the woman fingers. You remember I did tell you all about that one time? The foreman used to make joke with us good good. When the woman fingers chop out and he had to switch of the machine that was a different story. The woman bawling. Blood pouring like bucket all over the place. You think the foreman worried about her? He started cursing how he had to switch of the machine, losing production. He started on how these people stupid. If they can't read why they don't stay in their country or take job sweeping in the hospital. All kind of curse he cursing. Nothing about feeling sorry for the woman, nothing. The thing is it wasn't the woman fault. The day before the person that servicing the machine told them not to use that machine because something in it worn out and it had to be replaced. They let the workers use it and still blaming the poor woman.'

'As Mr Alvar said, if they did know something was wrong with the machine she should get a good piece of money from them. It's their fault, ent it, they should pay her.'

'America and England not the same.'

'I mean if they did know something wrong with the machine they should settle her up good.' Miss Alma was curious.

'Wasn't the same woman whose husband met us in Chapel market the Sunday we went to buy the confirmation dress to send down for Dorothy!' Uncle Dolphus reminded Aunt Sarh.

59

That must happened a long long time now. Because I remembered when Aunt Sarh sent down my confirmation clothes. I had twelve then. She send the dress and the veil and the money for Mammy to buy the shoes because she say she not sure if the shoes she see would fit me. Lord time pass quick yes. And one thing could make you remember other things you know. The day I confirmed a lot of rain fell in the morning. By two o'clock when time to go to the church everywhere dry. Jeanette for Miss Madonna was my confirmation sister. We was good good friends until we get big. When she went oversea first she used to write me. Is a long time I don't hear from her.

'Was he self? The same man?' Aunt Sarh went on.

'I remember him telling us that he went to collect his wife money the Friday. As soon as he opened his mouth to say who he was they handed him an envelope to take to his wife. When he said he wanted to speak to the foreman they said the foreman busy and anyway everything was in the envelope.'

'They settled her up then. They know was their fault they had to look after her,' Miss Alma added.

'Settle her Miss Alma? Settle her up? Dolphus you remember the man said when they gave him the envelope and said take it to his wife he thought was some kind of compensation in there. Instead when she opened the envelope was her P45 plus her pay and one week holiday pay. Just so they sacked her.'

'What! You mean she lose her job? They let her go just so? I never thought they could treat people like that.'

'Aaaye how you mean? I tell you they don't care. Two twos they get somebody else. They wanted to put another black woman on the machine without even repairing it. She quarrelled, quarrelled. She said she not going on that machine

60

until they had it fixed because everybody knew something was wrong with it.'

'I tell you Miss Alma if you can't stand up for yourself they walk all over you and still pretending to laugh with you. I never forget how that man take his farse self telling me to go and clean latrine. If I went there for cleaning job was something else. I tell you if I didn't get out of that place quick quick that morning I would of give that man one cuff in his mouth. Just one cuff and let them lock me up.'

'Lawd you hear thing about this England oui. This England is big. They have a lot of big business and things like that but . . . but I don't think I will like there you know . . . I don't think . . .' Devon did not finish what he was saying.

6

'Some things are nice. Even some of the people are nice. Is not all of them that treat you like rubbish.' When Aunt Sarh start about England she could go on forever. 'One day I coming from work. I passed by Danny shop in Barnsbury Road to buy two grain of banana and a piece of yam for our dinner. That time me and Dolphus just get together. I just turned into Cloudesley Road when bamp this little girl spit on me.'

'What!' Desiree shouted. 'You mean spit from her mouth she spit on you?'

'What you do?' Devon joined in. 'You didn't spit on her back? Eh Aunt Sarh? You didn't spit on her back? Heh, nobody spitting on me. I would just box them down.'

'Aaye I telling you. As I turned the corner she on the wall in front the house a little way from the bus stop. As soon as I reached up to her bamp the spit fly on my clothes.'

'Little or big they try to take advantage of you. She lucky. She know who she practising her nastiness with. When Sarh came home and told me I was ready to go behind her.' Uncle Dolphus was getting real vex. 'Child or no child if I was there the police would of picked me up. Is what they hear their parents say in the home. They think they could treat all black people like nothing. I tell you . . . heh . . .'

'Well as the spit left her mouth and fall on my coat I grabbed her off the wall,' Aunt Sarh grabbed Devon who was nearest to her, demonstrating how she grabbed that little girl. 'I didn't hit her yet she started crying saying she sorry. You could of seen she did it by spite. She was about seven but knew full well what she was doing. As I grabbed her she started shaking. "Wipe it, wipe it now," I said. That time my mouth full up of spit ready to land in her face if she made one vouse. I had on one of those plastic rain mac over my good coat. When I saw the spit running down on it I told her to take her hand and wipe it first, then I gave her a tissue to finish cleaning it.'

Aunt Sarh telling us the story but you could see Uncle Dolphus real vex you know. Perspiration pouring down his face. Tip, tippity tippity tip a tap, his fingers started playing music on the table. 'I tell you if was me, if was me,' he repeated, 'police would of picked me up that evening. Child or no child nobody spitting on me Adolphus Powell, no body. As the spit hit me the palm of my hand would of landed across her mouth . . . damn farse.'

'You box her now is you police arresting. You they pitching the cell,' now Aunt Sarh started playing her music with the plates and spoons. 'Come come clear the table, the food ready,' she announced in the same breath. 'Time for you to eat Dolphus. Time to get something in you belly before gas full you up.' I think Uncle Dolphus belly agreed with her because ruck cruck cruck turk ruck it answered.

'You see the same thing I saying. You hear your stomach? Come Dorothy, come and help me set the table. You eating here.'

I was thinking of taking the food home because I was not really hungry but when that callaloo soup hit my nose I couldn't wait. Anyway was the same food Mammy was cook-

63

ing. I don't think I'll bother bringing food down tonight. Is so we stay we always bringing food and little things for each other. Any little thing we have we exchange. Not really exchange, just share. Not just the family but neighbours and friends as well. Like if something scarce and Mr Alvar or Miss Alma have, they will send one for Aunt Sarh no matter how small it is. The same if Uncle Dolphus have fig and he know one of us don't have he'll send a hand for us to cook. And no matter what part of the island you living since bus passing is the same thing. You call the conductor give him a bag to drop say in Happy Hill. Since the bus passing that way is no problem. All he does when the bus reach in the person gap the driver blow the horn and the conductor put the bag down in the road by the gap. They could even drop it in the police station for that person and they'll get it.

One day we sitting downstairs cooling out and talking when we heard Comfort blow and Terry call out. I went by the road and picked up the little bag he dropped. While we were talking Aunt Sarh was saying is a long time she hadn't had a nice potato pudding, potato so scarce. When she opened the bag the conductor dropped I see water pouring out of the old lady eyes.

'What's the matter Aunt Sarh? What's wrong?' My heart started beating when I see she crying just like that. 'Look,' she pushed the bag in my hand, 'look we just sit down here talking about potato pudding and see hah. See what Miss Effie send. God bless her. Look what she send for me ... potatoes, tannia and two dasheen. God bless her and that boy she have dey.'

'Aaaye. You know is so the lady is. She know how you like you potato. If she get in the garden she will send for you. She is a good good lady.' I couldn't see why that made Aunt Sarh cried. It was normal.

64

'Sarh oye,' Uncle Dolphus called. He was coming from changing the goats he had tied under the pear tree down by the bay. 'Sarh oye what Comfort drop dey?'

'Something Miss Effie send up, some potato and things. Aunt Sarh so happy she crying,' I answered but killing myself laughing because I thought it was funny.

'You don't understand Dorothy. You don't understand at all,' Aunt Sarh went on to explain. 'They always on about how we backward. Some of our own people turning and call us small island to make us feel bad. I live over twenty years in England and there is nothing like that. Nobody give you anything for nothing. You have to dig in your purse for every single thing you want, everything. The shop keepers and them they looking at you plum in your eyes and thiefing you. Everybody is for themself. I think if they could charge you for saying howdy they'll charge you. Could be another reason why people afraid to say good morning. They 'fraid you go stretch your hand for payment.'

I laughed. 'Aunt Sarh you could say some funny things oui. How much you go pay for "a good morning"? Eh ten cents?'

She laughed. 'I telling you Dorothy here we people bad mouth and some hypocrite. Nobody farse in people business like Grenada people but we not selfish. We help out one and other. We look after one and other. In England everybody is self self self. I, me, I, as long as I am all right zafey they other person. And our own people becoming just the same. Dolphus used to say is the air. England air that turning people so. You think anybody will think of sending something for me for nothing. You see the water come in my eyes. I know why. I know. Anyway, come on girl. We making a bad potato pudding this evening, a bad bad potato pudding. She send tannia an all to put in it.'

Her face happy like the full moon. Sometimes in my mind

I try to see a picture of her in England especially when it make cold the way she would tell us. Tight up tight up in those heavy big clothes. Here she always so jolly. In house she always wear big floppy frocks, light and free. First thing in the morning like everybody she would open all the windows wide. It must of been very hard to get used to England from the stories she and Uncle Dolphus telling us. Like they had no kind of freedom. Natural freedom like. All that was going through my mind when I decided to have my callalloo soup now. I think we very lucky.

'Dorothy what do you girl? I talking to you you look as if you mind far away. You eating now?' Aunt Sarh asked again.

'Yes. Is the same callalloo Mammy cooking home. I go eat up here and if I hungry when I go home I'll eat again.'

'She did get salt beef by Mr Magnus. I hear he had fresh ones.'

'Chupes. Mr Magnus thing ever fresh. Nuh when I went to town yesterday I got salt beef and piece of salt pork. Mammy say she want the pork to put in some pease.'

'So Dorothy you having you aunty callalloo with salt pork, then go home for your mother callalloo with salt beef. Girl you greedy oui,' Miss Alma laughed. 'I got some nice salt mackerel from Mr Barlo this morning. He just got it from the boat. I'll cook up that tomorrow. You could pass by me.'

'Woye, salt mackerel, with coconut oil, fig and dasheen, woye.'

'All right, Devon. I'll leave piece of food for you too. You this boy.'

'Paren. Paren Dolphus.' Gordon called from below the breadfruit tree in the corner by Mr Eddie land. 'Paren Dolphus oye. Nenen Sarh howdy howdy.'

'Aye aye Gordon what you doing dey?' Miss Alma answered. 'What you doing dey in that hot sun? You is a man who don't like working in the sun. I thought you does start early to finish when the sun get hot.'

'Aaye Miss Alma I didn't know you by here. I just passing by the bay and I say let me pass by my godfather and godmother a little. Nen Sarh you awright?' He made his way under the window.

'Gordon! Long time I don't see you. I hear you busy in the garden you don't have time for us. Still it good you working hard to mind your children. We just eating. You want food?' Aunt Sarh offered.

'Lawd Miss Dolphus you ever hear Gordon refuse food? Food is this man middle name,' Miss Alma teased.

'Come come; pass on the stairs,' Uncle Dolphus told his godson. 'You just in time. You know when your neanen put the pot down.' Gordon was not really their godson but Aunt Sarh is his mother's godmother.

Gordon sat on the step leading from downstairs. Aunt Sarh handed him a bowl of soup. For a few minutes the only sound was the spoon and the bowl, the spoon and teeth. Then Miss Alma laughed.

'Bunjay Gordon take you time and eat nuh. You swallowing the hot food as if police behind you.'

We all turned looked at the young man, sweat pouring down his face like he just came out of the sea. The sweat was making a kind of pattern down his face and tracking down his jersey.

'The food sweet man . . . that callalloo sweet . . . and those dumpling; woye only my neanen could make that kind of dumpling,' Gordon laughed.

'Aaaye I thought you did something and police was behind you,' Miss Alma teased again.

'Police! Police!' Uncle Dolphus repeated. 'He lucky he not

67

in England. You don't have to do nutting for police to pick you up. Nothing.'

'How you mean, Paren . . . you joking? How you mean they just pick you up for nutting? You must do something. The police not mad to look at you and arrest you if you don't do nutting,' Gordon was surprised.

'Joking. He not joking. Tell them nuh Dolphus. Tell them. In England they arresting you for nothing. Just because they don't like you face. You face don't fit. Your colour upsetting them,' Aunt Sarh added.

'Is true true. That happening all the time . . . aaye that's nothing new,' Uncle Dolphus took up the story. 'When they want to pick you up they make up all kind of story. Sometimes you lucky if is only they arrest you. There was this boy they picked up once, young healthy young man. They picked him up near Ridley Road market because they said he looked like someone who will commit robbery.'

'What you mean, Paren? He look like someone who go thief so they locking him up before the person do the thiefing?' When Gordon said that everybody laughed.

'Something so. Well they picked up this strong healthy young man the next thing the family get message that the boy dead.'

'Dead! You mean they kill him Mr Dolphus?' Miss Alma almost choked on the piece of dumpling in her mouth. 'Bunjay, look at my trouble nuh. Look at these poor people trouble nuh.'

'Miss Alma, you hear anything yet,' Uncle Dolphus continued. 'You hear anything! Heh! They picked him up saying he looked like someone who will commit robbery then beat him to death in the station. I hear at first they did not even want his parents to see the body because it covered in blows. The other thing, the doctor who looked at the body just as

68

wicked. He said the boy died from natural cause. What natural cause could give him marks on his body as if they beat him with bootoo? Is the baton mark. The baton they beat him with. One of them mouth slipped. Somebody heard him say that they had to restrain the boy because he was under drugs. I hear that boy did not even smoke a cigarette; not a cigarette. That's not the first time they picking up innocent people in the road. There was another time these three young men coming from church. They had their Bibles in their hand going on and they were chatting about their work in the church when a police van pulled up besides them. The first policeman came out and asked them where they coming from. Aaye aaye the boys said they come from church and they going home. The police started questioning them. The next thing that happened was the policeman got on his phone and called others. Two twos a whole load of police cars surrounded those young men.'

'What happened then?' I asked.

'What happened but they throw the boys in the back of the van and take them to the police station. Not only that they beat them up that two of them ended up in the hospital. The young men came from church they ended up in hospital.'

'Bunjay! Uncle Dolphus how these people could beat you up if you come from church? They beat you up for praying to Jesus . . . aaye aaye,' Desiree, who was enjoying her food, stopped eating.

7

In Grenada religion is a way of life. Come Sunday and you don't go to church, it don't matter which church you follow, if you don't go and worship people call you 'beast'. My grandmother used to say only 'beast' don't know God. There are so many different different religion in the place I does think Grenada must be the ladder to heaven. Sometimes the stories you hear about some of the preachers is too much. Still when you go and worship you feel good inside you. You feel as if your spirit is free. This England must be a funny place . . . funny funny place. When Aunt Sarh first came home she said one of the things she missed in England was her church service.

'I used to miss my church bad bad. You know how we used to go and clean up the church on Saturday evenings? Dress up the altar and things like that for mass on Sunday? And the choir; I loved singing in the choir. I really missed that.'

I was telling Aunt Sarh that was quite in Grenville cousin Mamma had to send to get two yards of white taffeta to make Desiree dress for Christmas. Was then I asked her if she used to buy a new dress for Christmas like we do in Grenada . . . a new white dress for Christmas morning. It was the same time she told us about how she loved Sunday market. I don't remember what exactly started the conversation but I remember her face went very sad. As if a veil cover it when she said how she missed her church. Like she sorry and asking God to forgive her.

'It don't have church in England?' I asked then.

'It have church there yes but I never felt comfortable in there,' she said. 'Never. The first Sunday I dressed up, picked up my hymn book say I going to church. I feeling good. The church was just across the road from where I was living. That was after I left cousin Agnes place. I couldn't live with that woman at all at all. Was a good thing I had other family in England. I landed in England the Thursday evening. Papa Bunjay oye that was an experience, that was an experience. Mr Philip, that's cousin Agnes husband came to meet me in Heathrow. I expected cousin Agnes. When I followed everybody outside I see people come to meet their relative I don't see cousin Agnes. I started to get frightened. The next thing I heard this man called my name and stretching out his hands to me. I looking in his face because I didn't recognised the person. He stood in front me talking the same time I noticed a policeman watching us and kind of edging himself nearer. The man talking but I still looking for cousin Agnes. Was when he took out a photograph of cousin Agnes that I paid attention to him. He said he was cousin Agnes husband. By that time the policeman was standing right in front us. Anyway, Mr Philip said that cousin Agnes went to work and she asked him to come and meet me, but she will be home by the time we reach. I said thanks but still not too sure. He said the policeman was keeping an eye on him if I said I didn't know him he would of been arrested. I felt kind of glad because I thought I had some kind of protection especially when you hear so much stories about what happening to young girls and women travelling on their own to these big countries. Anyway, we collected my things to go home. Well I was lost. It was like I was in another world. Not just another country. Motor cars . . . so much motors . . . fast fast one minute, the next nothing moving. Not just cars but trucks and those big red vehicles. And those buildings, well that was something else. All of them join up join up. Like in town you have Everybodys Stores and the other stores together, was so, but all the houses were like that. I thought they were special buildings. Perhaps factories or hospitals the way all of them join up join up. I kept looking at them and thinking these houses don't have any nails in them. I was tired. I kept closing my eyes. Every time I opened them I see those big red vehicles so I asked Mr Philip what they were. "That's our bus," he laughed, "the English bus. The double-decker buses."

'What you mean double-decker?'

'They have upstairs and downstairs,' he tried to explain. 'Never mind, you soon get the hang of things.'

'Hm, soon get the hang of it, I had to learn overnight.' When you see Aunt Sarh start her stories she really go on, you know. She start one story and before she finish it she tell you about three stories in one.

'I had to learn overnight,' she repeated. 'The buses were funny with their upstairs and downstairs. Bus moving people walking inside. And they don't have names like "Tender Love" or "God is Love" you know, they have numbers. Like number 38 running from Leyton down the Lea Bridge Road to the Angel on to Victoria . . . like that. The motors was one thing, the roads another. So many roads and they so wide. Motors driving three and four alongside each other. One minute you on the main road next a twist there and turn here. Mr Philip said he taking short cut to beat the traffic but there was heavy traffic everywhere as far I could see. I thought the traffic strange, I was in for a bigger shock. When Mr Philip pulled up in front a house and told me we home I thought he was joking. Not joking laughing, but joking teasing. The building was like all the others but these not only upstairs and downstairs they tall tall. I had to bend my neck to the sky to see the roof. When he opened the door inside dark as dark night although the sun shining outside. He took my suitcases while I carried the boxes and other little things I had. Mr Philip started climbing stairs. Up the first flight then another. All I could see was closed doors. I started to wonder if this man is cousin Agnes husband for true because I expected my cousin to show her face by now, but nothing. When he reached on the second floor he turned back to see if was still behind him. This time I tired . . . I tired. He said we soon reach they living on the third floor. I tell you was only about three hours I put my foot in England but I was ready to catch the plane to come back home.

'The whole place feel funny funny. Like not a real place. All the time cousin Agnes writing she never said anything about living in a house that feel and look like Richmond Hill Prison only higher. Not only her but others as well when they write home or send photograph it's always how they happy in their work and the photographs always in pretty pretty flower garden so I couldn't understand where this man was taking me. Lord, I thought that was bad, I still had more shock waiting for me.

'My cousin Agnes was something else. From the time the woman put eyes on me she swell up. I had the feelings she didn't expect a big woman. I don't know. She asked me about home and the family but was as if she didn't really want to know. She was sort of stand-offish. I felt as if I dropped from the sky. The place where she lived was just one biggish room and a little box room where the children slept. She put me to sleep with the two children. If she was friendlier it would of been different. I would not of felt so bad but Bunjay oye I don't know. I don't know. England could really change people. Cousin Agnes wasn't the same person we knew at home at all. Not just that, she wasn't not the person who wrote those letters. She encouraged me to come to England. I didn't really wanted to leave home but I thought the experience will be good so I'll go for about three years and then come back.'

'Three years. All of us say we going for three or five years, when we reach in that place as if we catch up in a kind of trap. All how we say we going back home year in year out we stick in that place,' Uncle Dolphus interrupted his wife. 'Some of us never make it back. We leave our bones cover under snow.'

'That's true. We all say we only spending a little while, but to tell you the truth if I had follow my mind I would of been back in Grenada in no time at all. To tell you the truth even when Mr Philip took me inside the room I was thinking we only passing, we will be going to the proper home later. I learn quick.

'I was in for more surprises when I realised that all those closed doors I passed on my way up those those stairs were other people home. So many people living in that one house. At first I thought was family or friends visiting. In Grenada we had our little house sometimes with only one bedroom but is only we and our family and perhaps friends that living there but in England all kind of people living in one house. Sometimes the person that owns the house living in only one room with his wife and children and rent out the rest of the house. Sometimes the landlord don't even live in the house. Renting the rooms to make money on poor people back. They renting one little room for how much. You working for £8.00 a week if so much and you have to pay £3.10

74

shillings for one little room. Sometimes you have to catch water in the toilet. I was living in a Greek man house once. Two rooms I renting not a sink in the room. I had to catch bucket of water in the toilet and there were some people living in the house Lord they nasty. The toilet stink. They using it you think they will clean the place and is the same place they getting water to drink. I used to hold up my bucket over the sink to catch water although I used to bleach and disinfect the place before I use it. Every week I buy a big bottle of bleach and a big bottle of Dettol to clean the place. You paying so much for a place to live and you still have to mix up with all kind of people even in the kitchen. If you forget your things in the kitchen other people use it and turn around and curse you.

'I see some things in that England, you know,' Aunt Sarh sort of laughed. 'Talking about all kinds of people using the one kitchen, one day my friend Mary was sick in bed. I don't remember what was wrong but anyway me and Sonia, that's another friend, went to look for her and to do little things for her. I said I'll clean the room while Sonia went in the kitchen to cook something. Bunjay oye I never see this in my life. People could poison themself easy easy and don't know. Me and Mary in the room Sonia in the kitchen. A little while afterwards Sonia came up with a pot in her hand. I looked at her and noticed the creases under her eyes heavier. "What's wrong Sonia?" I asked. "Your face like something attacked you in the kitchen." She hold out the pot to Mary without saying anything. Mary in the bed let out one laugh. That must of been the first time she laughed in days with her sickness. When I heard her laugh I went and looked in the pot. Well I don't know. Mary laughing, but I was frightened. I think Sonia was frightened too. She put rice on the fire, as soon as it started to boil it turned blue. That's why I say

75

people could poison themself and don't know. The rice water blue blue as when you put blue in white clothes. Mind you, it was good to see Mary laughing. It turned out the pot Sonia used was not Mary's pot. Was the Pakistani man in the basement back-room pot. It was the pot he used to mix the dye to dye his turban.'

'Turban! What is turban Aunt Sarh?' Desiree asked.

'It's the hat the Pakistani people wear. Not a hat like a hat, more like a big headtie. I tell you all kind of people could be living in the house with you.'

'Is so I hear oui,' Miss Alma added. 'The same thing my sister tell me when she come on holiday from America. She said some of those people in the house she couldn't even understand what they saying. She said everytime she had to cook she feel bad.'

'Aaaye, saye saye I tell you this thing used to hurt me so much. You know me. I very particular. Miss Alma you didn't know me when I was young. I was very particular you know,' When Aunt Sarh repeated the 'very particular' Uncle Dolphus cleared his throat – em em. Turned and looked at his wife a kind of 'I-know-what-you-mean' look.

'How you looking at me so, Dolphus? Is true. I didn't used to mix up with any and any body. Then I had to mix up with all kind of people. Sometimes you in the kitchen some of them come peeping in your pot. One day I had to give an African woman a piece of my mind. These African and them too damn farse. What she come peeping in my pot for I don't know. I tell her never forget herself again.'

'You did still dey in the same house with your cousin Agnes?' Desiree asked.

'Chile I didn't stay in that place. I couldn't stay there at all at all. Was a good thing Mamma was a popular person and people remembered her kindness. Everest, that's my grand

76

aunt godson, those children who usually use the house down by the bay when they come on holiday, their father. Well he came to see me the week after I landed on the Sunday. I think he came more to see if I brought rum to give him a drink. When he saw where Cousin Agnes had me sleeping and when I told him about what happened when I went to have a bath . . .'

'In the bath Aunt Sarh! What happened in the bath?' I was curious. Although I hear people with different stories about England I used to think they making them up, but since Uncle Dolphus and Aunt Sarh came and telling us about how they lived in England I was more and more curious. 'What happened to you in the bath, eh, what happened?'

'Well I tell you,' she continued as she sipped the cold passion fruit drink. 'I landed the Thursday. That night cousin Agnes showed me this big deep long white basin and told me it's the bath. That's where I had to bathe. There was this contraption with pipes running inside it hanging over it.'

'Contraption'? Miss Alma laughed 'What kind of contraption Miss Dolphus?'

'It's this thing they called an "ascot". I can't even describe the thing. You put a shilling in a tin, to get the gas to heat up the water and also for you to cook. You had to push the money in a little slit in this thing turn a knob and the money fall inside it, like when you putting money in a money box. People used to break open this thing and thief all the money. When gas board come to empty it no money. Sometimes the landlord find it break open and call the gas board. Lord it had some thief in England oui. Anyway, when she showed me I only had a wash. Friday I did the same because I was not used to the climate. By Saturday I was feeling dirty so I said I will like to bathe. Cousin Agnes showed me how to to operate the ascot and told me to try to get my bath before

77

the other people got up and used up the money. I got my towels and things together. Mind you that time all my things were pushed in a corner and under the children bed. All cousin Agnes wanted to know was what I brought for her and if I had any money. Anyway about the bath, there was this pipe leading from the "contraption" hanging over the bath, you know like a shower but without the proper head and not as high as a shower. Well I went and stood up in the bath and sort of stoop right under the pipe and turned on the water. Lord Miss Alma I tell you the hot water hit my back . . . hot hot hot water hit my bare skin. Those children thought it was funny. They rolled about laughing.'

'So you cousin didn't tell you was hot water! I don't think she liked you otherwise she would of made sure you understand how to use the pipe.'

'She . . . that woman. I tell you when the hot water hit my back I jumped out you will think police behind me, pull on my dress and shouted for her. Was then she told me that I had to full up the bath of hot and cold water and sit down in it to bathe.'

'Bunjay,' Christine, the quiet one, shouted, 'bunjay Aunt Sarh you mean you had to sit down in that basin of water and bathe? If you could of full the basin of water have a sponge down then pour the water over you it would of been better but the way you saying you will be bathing in your own dirty water, bunjay oye, I never hear that yet.'

'Yes, Aunt Sarh how you could bathe in your dirty water? Lord that is nasty oui,' Desiree added.

'Nassteeeey. Bunjay oye you don't hear nothing. Nasteeey. If some of them nasty. You see mothers in the street with little children. If the child face dirty thupe they spit in the kerchief and wipe the child face.'

'Aunt Sarh you mean they washing the children face with

78

the spit from inside their mouth? The children must smell fresh,' Devon had to put in his bit.

Aunt Sarh refilled her glass of juice, added some ice. 'If I was to tell people about the things I saw in England I could sit down here until Christ come for his world.'

'I think you should write a book Miss Dolphus about these things, you and Mr Dolphus. Two of you should write a book,' Miss Alma stressed.

'True Nenen. You and Paren could write a book about England. You'll make a lot money.'

'Chupes; what book you talking about? What I know to put in book! People have to go in big big school and university to write book. Me and Dolphus just saying things we see happen in England. Nothing to put in book.'

8

Aunt Sarh got up and started clearing the table. 'What you doing with yourself when you not in bush?' she turned to Gordon.

'Liming woman. What you think he doing but chasing woman? I hear he all up in Grenville by my sister playing sweet man,' Miss Alma did not give Gordon a chance to open his mouth.

He rolled his eyes at the woman. 'Don't bother with Miss Alma Nenen don't bother with her at all. I have my children to mind I don't have time to chase other woman. Miss Alma don't make joke so man. Don't make these kind of joke. If Marcia hear you she kill me clean clean. I don't have time for that kind of thing.' He glanced sideways at Uncle Dolphus. Their eyes clashed. Both faces covered in a veil of mocked innocence.

'Chupes; all you man all the same. All you eyes too long. Never satisfy with what all you have. Never satisfy.' Aunt Sarh turned into the kitchen. She had noticed the exchange of glances between the men.

Uncle Dolphus moved to the front verandah. The sun had vacated its position and was now slowly sliding its way towards the horizon. The few drops of rain that fell earlier only served as a stimulant for the heat, so that even the birds had gone to find shade. Everything was quiet. Quiet and peaceful. Uncle Dolphus flopped in his favourite chair. The bamboo creaked as his bottom made contact. He picked up an old newspaper which was lying nearby and fanned himself. 'Lord it make hot,' he muttered. Miss Alma sat on the white plastic chair at another side of the verandah. Gordon joined them. He sprawled full length on the floor. Everyone relaxed. Now and again someone called from the road or from a passing vehicle. Lappa whined as a lizard disturbed his sleep under the rose bush in the gap. Bingo had gone with Devon down by the sea. Me and Christine went into the kitchen to clean up. We could hear Aunt Sarh tumbling in the bedroom. Tumbling, tumbling. My Aunt never rests. She always finding something to do, things that don't really need doing. She forever beating herself and complaining how she tired. She always tired. Uncle Dolphus does say she born tired. Anyway she like work because I tried to do most of the heavy work, and the others do what left to do, like sweeping the yard and thing like that, still my aunt finding things to tumble tumble.

That is one main reason why we come up every day so that my aunt could rest. But not my aunt, she don't know that word. I think is all that England running that still in her blood after all these years. When they first came I couldn't keep up with Aunt Sarh when we went out. She walking fast fast as if police behind her. One day when I was working in the health centre in town she came and meet me. Because was my half day she told me to bring up her message for her she going round River Road to see somebody. I get on 'Tender Love' to go home thinking my aunt will take the bus to River Road. I tell you by the time the bus reached by the fish market was my aunt I see round round rolling under the flamboyant tree going towards Queens Park. The speed she going with you think the jailer behind her. So she is still. All day long she doop dooping in the house finding work to do. Uncle Dolphus slow down quite a lot. Now he only do a little here and there, look after his animals and plant his food. With those boys and them helping him he just take things easy. Sometimes he has to quarrel with his wife to sit down a few minutes. The strange thing is she always on about how she used to run in England. How she used to be sleeping and running. The eyes closed but the mind running to catch with tomorrow. She in Grenada and she still running. I think there is still snow in the head.

'Aye aye everybody sleeping,' Aunt Sarh came on the verandah. 'Lord it make hot,' she fanned herself with her old straw hat.

'Aye Nenen come and cool out. It make hot come and cool youself. I want to go back and finish the piece of yam ground but I can't make it in that sun. Perhaps later.'

'So when you not working in the bush what you doing eh Gordon?' Aunt Sarh sat down on the empty chair opposite her dozing husband.

'Me? This and that. Nothing much. You know you godson always hustling to make a living. Carnival coming up soon I trying to get a band together and things like that. The last carnival we didn't do too bad but some of the band gone oversea or going so I have to look for new people. We must win first prize next year. That's what I am aiming for . . . first prize in the parade.'

'What you playing as this time?' Uncle Dolphus half opened his eyes.

'We don't really know yet. I will be something quite spectacular, quite spectacular, 'Gordon emphasised.

'Aye aye Gordon you have big word in your mouth oui. Whey you get them from? Who you taking lessons from?' Miss Alma teased.

'Ha ha hee hee hee,' Aunt Sarh started laughing. Everybody looked at her. 'I just study the time I went to carnival in England.'

'I didn't know you used to go and jump up in England. Paren Dolphus you never said my godmother used to play mas in England.'

'Behave yourself boy. I went to watch not play. Me! I don't have time to go and make pappyshow with myself. Was the first year me and Dolphus together. Every year they having carnival in Notting Hill I never put my foot in the place, especially when you see what happening on the television. You looking for mas and was more policeman you seeing than anything else. Sometimes the television camera picked up some hot steelband when you looking for the band and people dancing was police you seeing spoiling everything. I know they must be there to make sure things run all right. To keep those damn thieves and troublemakers in order because some of those hooligans only go to make trouble. Waiting as soon it start to make dark to come out but still there used to be too many police . . . too many of them. That year Dolphus coaxed me to go with him. I must admit I really enjoyed myself. I laughed until I almost pee myself. I see some funny things that year. And just like when we have carnival down here you see all kinds of things selling same same so in England. Everybody want to to make a quick shilling. You should see those white eat hot curry and rice or eat real fry fish. They fry fish different to us. They don't clean and season how we do. One thing I noticed them enjoying was fry saltfish and bakes.'

'Miss Dolphus you mean people go quite in England selling fry saltfish and bakes? We same fry saltfish and bakes?' Miss Alma seemed wake up.

'Aaaye how you mean if is we same food? Jamaicans call it

fry dumpling but it's the same thing we have.' Uncle Dolphus added.

'Woye o yoye; fry saltfish and bakes in England carnival. What's about the cocoa tea? If they made the cocoa tea it should help warm them up,' Gordon burst out laughing.

'If somebody made it, it will sell,' Aunt Sarh added. 'That year they even had sugar cane selling. Cutting it up in joints and selling one little joint for 75 pence. Almost a whole pound, 75 pence for a little joint of cane. You could see the borak running through some of them. They even peeled it for the customers. I stand up watching this white man with a joint of cane. He bought it and didn't bother ask the stallholder to peel it. He was standing by the stall holding this piece of cane turning it up and down like a lead pencil. Next thing I see the man take his finger trying to peel the cane. I just stand there watching him. Everytime he get a little piece between his nails his nail broke off. Everytime the nail break he curse under his breath. All you could hear was bastard, bastard. It was so funny I started laughing. The mass and them was one thing but watching this man peeling cane with his fingernail was something else.' Water was pouring down Aunt Sarh face you would think it was something that happening now or happened yesterday instead of those years ago.

'Didn't you show him how to peel it Aunt Sarh?' I asked.

'Show him. Show him what?' Uncle Dolphus answered. 'I was watching this mass playing Idi Amin when I looked around I see my lady killing herself laughing. When I looked good good was this man she laughing at. This time his face as red as when the sun going down. I felt sorry for him. I show him how to peel it, but said it is a bit hard so he should ask the stallholder to do it for him. The man looked at me and said the cane looked like dried bamboo shoot. After he spend all that time trying to peel it with his fingers then he turned and say it's dried bamboo shoot. Well I never. I left the stupid man and went to enjoy the jump up.'

'All the years I spend in England was the first and only time I see people making ice cream like we do here,' Aunt Sarh took up the conversation.

'You mean they don't have ice cream in England?' Devon had joined us.

'You look after the animal boy?'

'Yes Uncle Dolphus. I full up the pig basin. Eh, Aunt Sarh I thought England had everything.'

Aunt Sarh laughed. 'Of course there is ice cream. More than anybody could eat but they make it in big machine. There is no ice cream can like we have down here. You don't see people turning turning till it ready. Everything is done by electricity. Was in the carnival I saw people making it like us. The thing taste good. Not like the usual England ice cream that taste like wet flour. Some even look like soap fraught. But with our ice cream you could taste the real thing. These people who was selling it must make some good good money that year. You should see the crowd around them. They had two can when one selling the other turning.'

'What's about snowball? If they don't know our ice cream they don't know snowball, eh Aunt Sarh? I don't mean when the snow falling an thing like that. I mean snowball like we make.' That Devon asking question worse than a lawyer and the things he does come out with. I don't know. When the boy get big he must turn lawyer.

'Snowball,' Aunt Sarh laughed. 'Snowball. It's hard to get the big block of ice to make shave ice, but once they had it in Ridley market. Was the year of the hot hot summer. I don't know where they got those blocks of ice but you should of seen how people flocked around them. The boys enjoyed themselves shaving the ice as well. It kept them cool.'

85

'You mean the time when there wasn't water and the people in charge told everybody to bath together? I remember you telling us about that,' Miss Alma added.

'Was the same same year . . . hmm, hmmm. You have any juice in the fridge Sarh?' Uncle Dolphus enquired.

'Dorothy go inside and see what's there give Dolphus you hear. If the juice finish take a bottle of ginger beer downstairs.'

'It make too hot, I don't want ginger beer.'

'Don't worry Uncle Dolphus. I'll make some lime juice. Aunt Sarh, is that all right?'

'Of course that's all right. Put some linseed essence in it.' I left them and went in the kitchen to prepare the lime juice.

I love going up to Aunt Sarh's. Listening to the stories reminds me of when I was young and taking out nansi stories in the night or on Fridays at school. The old people love telling stories as well. It must remind them of when they were small too. Once Aunt Sarh said one thing she enjoyed since she came home apart from everything else was how we were able to sit down outside on the step and talk, especially on moonlit nights. Sometimes on the steps cooler than inside the house so even if it dark it doesn't matter. Aunt Sarh said in England you can't even leave your window open. One night that I remembered good good was All Saints' night two years ago. Outside pitch dark only lights were the candles on the graves that is where people bothered to put a light for their dead family. Aunt Sarh wasn't well that night so the rest of us went to the cemetery and she stayed home and burned candles on the step. Uncle Dolphus don't usually bother with burning candles for his people. He said his mother and father done dead and gone burning candles for them won't make them see God face if they didn't prepare their souls before they died. Aunt Sarh said is the devil in his skin. Since she know him he never kneel down and say a word of prayer;

she hope he prepare his soul. Anyway, that night when we came from the cemetery, was me, Desiree, Cynthia, cousin Agnes grandson and my two god children, that's Christlyn, Miss Mavis children, we heard Mr Alvar, Miss Alma, Aunt Sarh and Uncle Dolphus beating mouth on the step. The place dark. The candle lights were like fireflies dancing on the ground. You should hear the big laugh they letting go in the darkness. We joined them. They were eating asham, and potato pudding. Uncle Dolphus voice stronger than all the others. Aunt Sarh was telling them about how they used to cut off the electricity in England. She said sometimes was because the workers went on strike. 'Lord,' she said, 'without electricity to light up the place, the whole place dark like inside the whale that swallowed Jonah.' Mind you I think they turn their mouth when we joined them because of the children.

'Bunjay you say something oui Miss Dolphus? You could really say something. You ever see inside whale belly?'

'How you mean I could say something Mr Alvar? Is true. When they cut off the electricity everywhere pitch dark. Not one little firefly you seeing yip self. Only light on the road was the motor lights. All the houses in dark. After the first time that happened I made sure I went and bought a little lamp and put paraffin in it. When Dolphus met me I had two lamps, one in the kitchen one in the bedroom. When he saw them he laughed at me, saying I should use candles like everybody else. Me I don't like burning candles. They too dangerous . . . too too dangerous.

'True,' Uncle Dolphus put on his serious voice. We could see the outline of his face in the candle light. 'Plenty plenty people, young, old and even babies lost their lives in fire caused by candles. Not only candles that cause fires but that is one main cause. I know what Sarh saying. There was this

87

birthday party going on once somewhere in south east London. This woman made a birthday party for her daughter. The young people dancing and enjoying themselves good good just like that the house catch a fire. Up to now fire brigade and police saying they don't know how the fire started. Was somebody outside that set the house on fire. Jealous they jealous because those young people enjoying themselves.'

'Bunjay,' Miss Alma shouted. 'Bunjay Mr Dolphus anybody hurt?'

'Aaah Miss Alma; thirteen young people burn to death. Thirteen young healthy black people killed just so. The people children died and nobody answered for their death. I don't think that they bother to investigate the case properly up to this day.'

'Burn them to death! Set the house on fire because they jealous! Papa Bunjay people bad oui. I tell you people like that must have their own own hell. Their own own hell,' Mr Alvar rocked on the chair where he was perched in the corner. The flickering candle lights dancing across his face showed off his set jawbones.

'People really wicked in this world, really wicked,' Aunt Sarh added.

Everyone was quiet. The only sound was the crickets singing their goodnight hymns. It was as though without saying a single word we were together praying for those young black people who lost their lives in England. The silence only lasted a few minutes but it seemed like hours.

'Aaah. Mothers' children gone just like that. Just like that?' Uncle Dolphus added like an afterthought, 'I didn't used to go to much parties before but after that I was even more careful which party I went to. Although you could never tell. When wickedness take people they don't care who they hurt.'

'You used to go to fetes and things Aunt Sarh?' Cynthia

asked, 'I mean like Christmas fete? You used to go to fete on the beach?'

'Gal, you stupid oui. How Aunt Sarh will go to Christmas fete on the beach in the winter? You don't hear Uncle Dolphus does say how much clothes he have to put on him when cold bite him?' Michael, that's my godson, laughed at Cynthia.

'Well if not in Christmas there must be other fete. So you is the one that stupid. You that Michael always calling people stupid and you more stupid than everybody,' Cynthia was really vex.

'You used to go to fete and things Aunt Sarh? I bet you and Uncle Dolphus could really dance. Uncle Dolphus you used to go to fete with steelband and things by the sea like we do here, eh Uncle Dolphus?' Cynthia continued chattering.

'Chupes what sea? You think you seeing any sea in England girl?' Aunt Sarh answered. 'I loved going on bus party by the sea but it nothing like here. Everywhere you turn in Grenada you could see the sea. Even if you deep deep in the gully somewhere or high up in the mountain you just have to peep through the green bush or climb a tree and the lovely blue blue sea stretching all around. Not in England. You could live in that place all your life and don't set you eyes on sea water. If you lucky to go on trips to the sea the water always look grey and dirty like when rain fall down here and river come down.'

'What!'

'Aaye aye. What you mean what? I telling you I know people in London for thirty odd years and never see sea water. I don't mean that England don't have sea but it so far away that you have to go on bus party to get to the beach. The place big you know. Not like you just catching a bus and going down to Grand Anse. I used to go to Margate or one

89

of the beaches every summer. That was one place I really liked, Margate. The beach was cleaner than most places. London Transport used to run parties on Sunday for people who worked for them. I had this friend he was a conductor on the number 48 bus. He used to book for me and my other friends. Lord we had to drive far. The driver had to stop half way to rest and cool off the engine before we get to where we going. We used to leave the garage about nine o'clock in the morning by half past ten we'll be half way. Stop take a rest. Who want to go to toilet go to toilet before we off again. The same thing when we coming back. But I used to enjoy it. The only thing though the place used to pack up. Not like Grand Anse where you have place to move. Sometimes you have the beach and the sea just for you and the little fishes. There the place pack up. People lying down the beach you have to raise your foot and pass over them. They lie on the beach on towels as when people in hospital. The way the beds side by side in the big ward was just as how the people lie side by side on the beach.' Aunt Sarh took a sip of the lime juice. A shadow crossed her face. She shivered.

'You all right Aunt Sarh?' I looked at her closely.

'I all right Dot girl I all right.'

I looked at her for a few minutes. I was a bit puzzled. It was a long time since she'd called me Dot. When she was in England whenever she wrote or sent things she always called me Dot. Even when she came home, when everybody was calling me Dorothy, she called me Dot. I don't even know when she stopped. Hearing her call me Dot now puzzled me. 'You all right Aunt Sarh?' I asked again.

'I all right. As I talk about the hospital bed I remember when I worked in the hospital.'

'I didn't know you was a nurse Miss Dolphus. You never said that before,' Mr Alvar grinned, 'is a good thing you didn't let these Victoria people know otherwise before you know what happening they will put you down as the doctor on call. You will come Doctor Otway assistant.'

Everybody laughed. The things Mr Alvar comes up with is eh, the things he say. But is true though people just want to hear one little word and they make up stories you 'fraid.

'I worked in hospital when I went to England first. My first job was in the hospital in Liverpool Road in Islington. Not a proper nurse. There was plenty plenty black people working there at time. Quite a few working in the kitchen and general domestic work and others like me doing auxiliary nursing. It's like helping the nurses. The work was bad and not bad if you know what I mean. The hours was not bad. Sometimes I worked shift so I could work in the morning, go home and do my housework and then go back to work in the afternoon. Then part of the work was not so nice. You had plenty lifting. Lifting those patients. Some of them heavy. They like dead weight. I used to work mostly on the old people ward. Bunjay you had to put up with some things you know. Some of them can't do anything for themselves. You have to feed them, clean them, turn them and still they cursing you. Some of them telling you plain plain they don't want black people touch them. I remember one particular old white woman. The woman disgusting; she miserable. She gave everybody a hard time. Nobody wanted to look after her. She so miserable that after a time her family stopped coming to see her. There was this other Grenadian woman who worked on the ward with me. She was the most patient person on the ward. When everybody don't bother with the sick woman Miss Enid would look after. Well one morning it was too much.' Aunt Sarh rubbed the palm of her hand. She closed her eyes.

'Lord people could put other one in trouble. Put you in

91

trouble just so,' she continued. 'That old woman has every-body upset that morning. After eleven o'clock everybody resting she shouting. First she wanted a drink orange juice. I was going to attend to her but Miss Enid said she'll do it. She got the drink, then she wanted to sit up in the chair. Miss Enid helped her to get out of the bed. When Miss Enid handed her the glass of juice she said she don't want that, was milk she wanted. She had the other woman up and down the ward. Up and down like a little child. The last straw was when Miss Enid brought her the milk she started quarrelling that she asked for a cup of tea. Swearing that was tea she asked for. That's another thing, these people could lie easy. The first thing I learned from them was never tell them the truth. Never tell them your business straight if you have to tell them anything at all. Anyway Miss Enid brought her the tea. As she stretch her hand for the cup she started shouting how this black woman want to poison her. With that she dropped the cup of tea in her lap.'

'Bunjay oye! Poison. Miss Dolphus she didn't know what she was saying. The head old she losing her senses.'

'Losing her senses Mr Alvar. Losing her senses to put other people in trouble. I tell you how these people and them could lie. But wait nuh you hear the worse part yet. She dropped the cup and next minute without warning spaam she spit in Miss Enid face. Spit right in the woman face. I tell you Miss Enid was a very quiet person. She had a lot of patience. All the patients liked her but that was too much, too too much. The old woman had a bad chest. Always hawking up some thick nasty flame. She go spit in the person that cleaning her face, eh. Well a nurse was by the next bed but she couldn't move quick enough. As the spit splattered on Miss Enid face the full palm of her handed made contact with the old woman face. And she started bawling. Not the old woman, Miss Enid.

92

She started one piece of bawling you would think somebody was beating her. That morning I never see sister moved so fast. Nurses, sister even the porters everybody rushed to the ward.'

'What happened after that Aunt Sarh? Miss Enid lose her work?'

'She didn't lose it the same time because the nurse and others who saw what happened pleaded for her but they still cautioned her. They moved her to another ward. I worked in that place for about seven years until they closed down the hospital. They sent some of the workers to different hospitals but I didn't want to go. For one thing it would of been more travelling especially in the winter.'

9

Sometimes when they tell us these stories I could feel things running through my body as if I am in that place. Some of the things she says, not just she, Uncle Dolphus as well, is just the opposite to the way we are. Like that thing about funeral. I remember the first time she said about how people going to funeral in England. That night moonlight bright. We went round by Miss Mabel, that is Mr Alvar wife. Aunt Sarh hadn't seen her for a few days so she passed by her that night. I was sleeping up there that night so I went with her. I think why Miss Mabel stopped coming by Aunt Sarh as she used to was because she knew about Miss Alma and Mr Alvar, and she knew that Miss Alma always at Aunt Sarh. One day they had bacanal in Mr Duberry rum shop on the other side of Victoria bridge. I hear one bacanal. Miss Alma brass for so boy. Miss Mabel in the shop she go up in the other woman face and tell her to stop spreading news about how Alvar sleeping at her. People taking their two eyes and see Mr Alvar coming out of her house foreday morning for the woman to shut she mouth she making noise. Mr Alvar just as bad. When he by Aunt Sarh and Miss Alma pass they going on as if they didn't see each other for long long time. Anyway that night we by Miss Mabel she cooked one pot of oil down. We eat that breadfruit, coconut and corn meat for so that night eh. Was the sweetest piece of breadfruit I had for a long time. I don't really like breadfruit but in oil down I could eat three slices and just drink water. While we chatting Miss Mabel asked if we going to Mr Noble funeral in Waltham the next evening. Aunt Sarh said it depends on how she feels.

'I wonder if Tanty Clarita hear when the funeral is,' I said.

'Aaye how you mean if you aunt hear? You ever hear funeral pass that aunt you have dey,' Miss Mabel laughed. 'I never see a woman like a funeral so since I born. I never see that.'

That's true, you know. As soon as my aunt hear somebody dies she get out her funeral dress. She had one black, one white and one mauve especially for funerals. She don't have to know the person. She always says the person could be a family we don't know. That's another thing of all the sisters and brothers, that's my mother, Tanty Jane, Aunt Sarh, Tanty Clarita and my two uncles, only she alone knows the family tree. The person could be my great great grandmother sister grandson daughter second child, my aunt will find that person and tie them to the family. Don't ask me to break that down because I could never find the end. As I saying, she loves a funeral. As long as she could get a lift or she could walk that dead person sure of one mourner behind their coffin.

Swuueep, Aunt Sarh licked her fingers, 'That oil down good Miss Mabel, it good. I don't know how my sister would of made out in England you,' she laughed. 'The way she loved funeral so, she would starve. I don't mean for food, but just for going to funeral.'

'How you mean?' I asked.

'Well, England people funny you know. They not like us. I don't mean black people in England. We still have we thing in us. When we have sick and death we click together. We support each other. Not the white people. If they don't invite you to the funeral you better don't put yourself there.'

'What you mean, invite you?'

'Aye aye Miss Mabel I telling you they have their special people they invite to the funeral. Most times after they bury the body is fete they feting. I mean they have more fete in funeral than in wedding. If my sister up there I don't know how she go make it nuh.'

'When you say they having fete you mean for the wake and three days prayers they does have food and things?' Miss Mabel sister who was too busy eating at first to say anything joined in the conversation.

'What wake you talking about Miss Eslyn, what wake? They don't keep wake. You living in number 71 and a death in 69 you don't know. I know this old lady who lived next door to us in Bromfield Street when her husband died. We used to talk good so I thought I go by her for a little while. I was going to spend a couple of hours with her and whoever was there. When I rang the bell the house in half darkness. When she opened the door she alone in there. The body in the hospital and she alone sit down in there with her cat. I almost cried. Not for the dead but for her loneliness. But the strange thing is, is so they want it. When I told an African friend he couldn't believe it but he said these people them selfish anyway. Even in grief they selfish.'

'These people an dem funny oui, they really funny,' Miss Eslyn said, clopping the piece of salt pork.

'Funny; you think you hear anything. You know when we have dead how we bawl and bawl because of our feelings. I mean deep deep down we feel our lost. We know that person gone for good so we bawl.'

'Aye aye how you mean we bawl, Aunt Sarh, we bawl oui. Let Miss Mabel tell you about when my father died. I wanted to go too. When I look and see they putting the box down in that hole, is my father in the box the whole of inside me mix up, knot up, twist up . . . Jesus Christ . . . I don't know. If I couldn't bawl out to release what inside me I don't know what would of happened. When they cover George Mitchell in that hole I wanted them to cover Dorothy Mitchell too.' I started shaking as the tears full up my eyes.

'Never mind Dorothy, never mind. God knows best,' Aunt Sarh consoled me. 'That's the difference with us,' she went on, 'the difference between us and England people. They don't cry like us. You hear how I tell you they laugh "zooup, fliiip" across the mouth and done when they crying is even worse. You don't see eye water you know. All you hear is ouish, uish, ish, ouish, stifling in a kerchief.' She took the end of her dress and started dabbing the corner of her eyes.

'Bunjay oye look at my trouble tonight nuh, Miss Dolphus you good oui,' Miss Eslyn burst out one laugh. That started all of us laughing. 'How they crying, show us again.'

'Ouish, heeish, ish, hish, and dabbing the corner of their eyes with a kerchief tip tip tip. These people and them is something else. And I tell you some black people over there coming just like them. They don't know how to show their feelings. They think if they cry is shaming they shaming themselves. Some of them come so "white" they don't know if they black. I went to this funeral once. Was my friend from Nevis husband who died.'

'But Aunt Sarh you had friend from everywhere!'

'Aaaye how you mean? I tell you England is a mix up mix up place. You meet people from places in the West Indies you didn't even hear of before. Anyway the day of this funeral I see something I wanted to cry. I mean not cry for the dead man but because his people shame to cry. Even when they put the coffin in the grave not a drop of eye water fall in the grave self. Everybody stand stiff stiff like they meet up lajabless under the silk cotton tree. I looked at my friend you could see how she face full up like she drink soda. To tell the truth was like her whole head was swollen. It was the pressure she under. She under the pressure burying her husband but she shame to cry out to let go the thing inside her. You know the grief that tie up like a knot inside her if wasn't shame she'd just bawl out and let it go.'

'Shame to cry for her husband? What she shame for, eh Miss Dolphus, what she shame for? People could really turn stupidy when they travel to these big countries. I never hear that in all my life. Shame to show my grief.'

'Miss Eslyn the only little eye water I see that day was in the church when the man big daughter started crying. He had that child with another woman in Nevis before he and his wife married. They were together since in their country but you know how man eye long. Well is that daughter that in church crying for her father. She alone had little water in her eyes.'

'Aaaaye she cry nuh. After she not shame to show her feelings.'

'Wait nuh Miss Mabel you hear nothing. When she crying a cousin of hers was sitting next to me turned and said to me, "chupes what she bawling for eh hypocrite she hypocrite. Why she don't hush she mouth." "How you mean, hush she mouth?" I said. "Is she father she must cry for him." Right in the church that woman started telling me how she cousin hypocrite and bad-minded. How she think the father leave money in the bank and land in Nevis. That's why she bawling she think the mother-in-law go give her something. How all the time the man sick in hospital she never put her foot to see him, not even to wash a pair of pyjamas for him now he dead she come say she bawling. She better hush she mouth before somebody box out she teeth. Quite in the church you know. Quite in church she started bad-mouthing the cousin. I tell you I don't know what do we people. England change some of us for so. Some of them you know good good in Grenada. You and them grow up in the same place. You know their whole family when you meet them in England and hear them talk you only have to close your mouth. You and them come from right in Victoria but they never saying they from Victoria, always St Georges. They never say they from Grand Roy or Concorde, or places like that, always St Georges. People think St Georges is the only place in Grenada. I tell you the only time some of them ever put their foot in town was to get their passport. I wouldn't even say to catch plane because they didn't have to pass in St Georges to go to Pearls.'

'I think is the snow in their head that make them funny Miss Dolphus. Too much snow. It soak inside their brains, soak in their skull as when you soak dry pease.' Miss Eslyn always come out with something.

We sat down outside. Me and Miss Eslyn on the step in front of the house. Aunt Sarh plump her bam right in front the kitchen door and brace her back against the doorway. That is her favourite sitting spot whenever we pass by Miss Mabel. Only when it raining she'll go in the kitchen. Miss Mabel well glad for the company. She was telling us about how Mr Alvar behaving bad. She said Miss Alma too stupid if she think she is the only woman the man have outside. The man does go all the way down River Road behind a Dougla woman. Miss Mabel said she don't have time to bother with him at all at all. She said from creation man like that they would never change. Is woman to make them know their place. She not making sheself no pappyshow behind no man.

When we ready to leave Miss Mabel gave us a big roast

breadfruit. She said was for Uncle Dolphus because she know he likes it. Miss Mabel know what she saying. Uncle Dolphus love a roast breadfruit fry over in the morning with saltfish souse and cucumber, and wash down with a big cup of Milo. Aunt Sarh said in England she used to buy one little slice of breadfruit for how much money. Sometimes as much as £1.50 for a slice because they put everything on scale and weigh it. Just imagine 6 dollar and cents for a piece of breadfruit and when it plentiful here nobody want it. Not only that, she used to buy zaboucca just as dear. One little one for almost £2.00 sometimes it don't have a taste. Now she come home and these things all around the house. She said she wanted the things and she couldn't take bus to Grenada or put the money in pot to cook so she had to buy them.

'Miss Mabel oye I must go before we meet up lajabless under the silk cotton tree eh, so goodnight. Thanks for the breadfruit. Dolphus go enjoy it for so.'

'Goodnight Miss Dolphus.'

'Goodnight Miss Mabel.'

'Goodnight Dorothy. Tell Miss Beryl howdy for me tomorrow.'

It was about nine o'clock when we left Miss Mabel house. The moon was shining but not too bright. As we passed under the baoucanoe tree the moon was shining on the leaves like candles on the river when those Ducane people making salacca in the busherie. We were the only people around at that time. We strolled home. Although earlier Aunt Sarh mentioned the lajabless under the silk cotton tree we were not afraid. It was just a joke but I know some people who would not walk there alone day or night. There is always some saying or the other about the devil working under the silk cotton tree. Me, with all what they saying I never see anything and I walk under there night and day.

The night was very quiet. The only sound was the waves splashing on the shore, the crickets chatting to each other and sometimes a dog barking.

'I was just thinking about England?' Aunt Sarh broke the silence.

'You want to go back?' I teased.

'Go back. Me! Well perhaps for a holiday but that's all. Nuh I was just thinking when I in England you think you getting me outside this time of the night without Dolphus.'

'It not that late. Just people not passing down by here tonight. I think they up by the society hall in bacco.'

'I know it's not all that late but in England people so wicked you 'fraid to walk the road when it make night. In winter it worse because it make dark early and then when the fog come down it's even worse. It's like you walking through thick thick smoke. Can't see an inch in front of you. But was the wickedness that made me stay inside when night come. I glad to be inside my room and close the door. You walking the road and people attacking you for nothing. You don't tell them their eyes black or white yet they abusing you and if you don't look sharp beat you up as well. They so damn coward they never walk by the one that you could fight back always in a crowd. When Dolphus out I used to prayer hard until he come home.'

'They never interfere with Uncle Dolphus though.'

'Heh interfere with who! You Uncle Dolphus! After they not mad. He always say the day or night any of them touch him he making sure when the police come to pick him up the ambulance come to pick them up too. One night he came home, he vex. I never forget that night. You uncle vex and so he cursing. I had to coax him coax him to get him to calm down.'

'What happened? They attacked him?'

101

'Not him. He and this Indian man was at the bus stop. A crowd of those hooligan with their head clean like calabash come and started on the poor Indian man. They called him all kind of names. The more the man asked them to leave him alone the more they abused him. All that time Dolphus stand under the bus shed watching, waiting for them. Waiting to see what they will do when they finish with the man. He stand there not saying a word, but when he see they started pushing the man about he had enough. He said he pushed himself in the crowd and tell them if they put hand on this man tonight they have to fight him too. When they heard that and see him put his hand inside bag they started backing off. That time Dolphus was a big man. I mean he had the weight on his body; when he get vex and he swell up you better watch yourself. Those damn coward called him black bastard and run.'

'That man was lucky Uncle Dolphus was there.'

'Aaye; you telling me. When they gone he went up to Dolphus and thanked him. He said if he was alone he would of been sorry for his skin. Apparently was not the first time they beat him up. These clean head hooligans used to go about beating up Pakistani. They not stupid they know who they could bring their stupidness give. A West Indian man would burst their skin. With these kind of people about it wasn't safe in the night alone. Although I knew Dolphus could look after himself I still used to worry. I know those hooligan couldn't handle him. He was a big healthy man. He was hardly ever sick.'

10

That's something in truth, Uncle Dolphus hardly sick. Since they came down they never really sick. Sometimes they complain how the joints in the fingers and knees painful, especially Aunt Sarh. She had arthritis in all her joints sometimes they swell up big big. She say is the cold that soak through the vein. Sometimes I feel real sorry for them the way they complain with the pain all over their body, especially when the rain about to fall. Long before it set up Aunt Sarh could tell you rain soon fall. She says she could feel the joints biting her. She would show me how the knees swollen puffy puffy like when you mix yeast to make bread. Her fingers twist up twist up. Sometimes when she sits down the knees crack, crickety crick, worse when she ready to get up. She says it's woodworm that working in there. She makes me laugh. She could tell when the rain will fall by the way the joints playing up. Sometimes I tease her. Call her weather woman. Once I asked her if she didn't go to the doctor in England with it.

'Doctor Malik said that there is no medicine for arthritis,' she said.

Apart from that they never sick since they come down. Uncle Dolphus has the arthritis too but not as bad as Aunt Sarh. She said that's because she worked a long long in the factory washing and ironing clothes. All day long in the hot and cold, hot and cold. Taking out wet clothes from big machine and totting them straight in ironing machine. Was the same factory where she said a woman got her finger cut off and the foreman got vex because he had to turn off the machines.

'If I didn't leave that place perhaps I wouldn't be here today,' she told me one day. 'You working in the hot and cold, cold and hot every day, winter to summer. You inside this hot room all day, sometimes working right in the fire when zphuup in the evening you out in the freezing cold. You get up in the morning sun shining outside look nice and warm. You dress in light clothes as soon as you go outside and turn the corner, like you leave inside an oven and jump in a fridge. Sometimes you look at the sun it look tired. Like it take all the little strength in it to try to shine through the grey cloud. Dolphus strong you hear, he strong. The cold never used to bother him much.'

Since Uncle Dolphus come down, apart from the arthritis in his joints is only once I see him sick in bed. That was the time he had the bad fever. He had this hot hot fever all what Aunt Sarh did the fever wouldn't cut. He was just roasting up. When Tanty Clarita saw how he shaking on the bed and how he perspiring she started bawling how the man go dead. She on about how people come from the cold country their body full up of cold and they don't last long in the sun. When the sun heat boot up with the cold in the body it dry up the blood. I don't know where she does get the things from. When she saw that everything Aunt Sarh used the man didn't get better she told Aunt Sarh she hear that there is a good doctor in Barbados who know how to treat these 'English' people. Well, I never seen Aunt Sarh so vex in my life. Tanty Clarita is younger than the sisters and brothers but you would think she was the oldest. She not only saying she heard about the doctor but telling the sister that she must take her husband to Barbados. Telling her, you know, as if she don't have a mind of her own. I tell you Aunt Sarh vex, she vex. She started quarrelling. This time the mouth stretch straight from Grenada to England.

'All the time I in England I drinking my bush when I have cold. I boil the same same bush you send for me when Dolphus have cold. We never went to no doctor for things like that. The man have a little fever you talking about giving Bajan doctor my money. You Clarita, you does really talk some stupidness.' She turned on the sister. 'All the bush I used to ask all you to send for me what you think I did with them eh? What you think I did with them? In winter when everybody hold up with cold me and Dolphus hardly blow our nose. I used to boil the zaeberpick or coollie paw paw strong strong and we drink it as hot as we could bear it, one cup before we went out in the cold in the morning and one cup in the night before we went to bed. Quite in England is we bush I taking for medicine, now I here Dolphus have a little fever you come telling me about Bajan doctor. Chupes. You this Clarita too damn stupid you see, you too stupid.' Aunt Sarh quarrelling. Mammy killing herself laughing. Tanty Clarita standing by Uncle Dolphus bed with one hand cup her mouth and the other brace her belly.

'Aye aye Aunt Sarh I didn't know you used to really drink the bush we used to send for you. All the time Mammy and them used to dry them and send for you I didn't believe you used them. I always thought you had the best medicine in England.'

'Dorothy girl, I tell you these people and them clever. They know how to use their brains. They coming down here saying we backward because we still believe in this that and the other

105

especially we bush medicine then turn around and take the same same bush and make medicine to put on shelf . . . expensive expensive medicine. They taking the same things we have growing wild and make first-class drugs. When them come and see us using our things they running their mouths about how we believe in darkness making us forsake what we have then take our things and say they discover, they invent.'

'Is so it go Miss Dolphus? I didn't know!' Miss Alma said.

'How you mean is so it go. I tell you is just so. You see the paw paw we have down here kicking all over the place? Scientist now using it to treat cancer. The same same paw paw. I know what I saying.'

Anyway the second evening Uncle Dolphus still the same. All what they did no change. Aunt Sarh sent Devon and Desiree to pull some bush. She told them exactly what she wanted. She then boiled up a whole big pan of all these different bushes. The smell of this thing worse than obeah shop. When the bush well well boiled she and Mr Alvar gave Uncle Dolphus a bath with the mixture. The two of them stripped and bathe this big man, then wrapped him up in young fig leaves and gave him some of the same bush water to drink. You wouldn't believe but next morning early early Uncle Dolphus got up ready to go out to change his animals. The old man got up strong and hearty you wouldn't believe was the same person fighting fever the day before. That the only time I'd seen Uncle Dolphus sick. Aunt Sarh knew he could of looked after himself in England against these damn scamp and them but I suppose she still worried. Just imagine you 'fraid to go out if you want to.

We passed under the silk cotton tree. Aunt Sarh leaned against the sea wall a little. 'So you didn't used to pass by your friends in the evenings to beat mouth?'

She laughed, 'In England people don't have time to pass

by people, especially in the winter. Everybody busy busy trying to make life. Before I met Dolphus I only used to go by my family sometimes on Sunday. When I moved from my godson he used to come and pick me up to spend the day by them and in the evening bring me back. Then when me and Dolphus get together I used to go out with him sometimes but not all the time. I even went to the dogs a few times with him and his friend Jim. The thing is I didn't really like to go out much.'

I remember the time Uncle Dolphus talked about the dogs and how black men in England making horse eat all their money? He and Mr Alvar was sitting under the mango tree below the kitchen window by the track going down to the sea, just sitting there cooling off and brangoing. It must of been some old slackness they talking about because you should hear the big old laugh they letting go. As soon as me and Aunt Sarh reach there they changed their mouth. They think is stupid we stupid. Me and Aunt Sarh came from having a little dip in the sea. Aunt Sarh love she sea bath especially when sun splitting earth. She said when she in England she don't know what is sea bath now she home she enjoying the salt water. Uncle Dolphus does say the salt helps to melt the snow in his blood. When me and Aunt Sarh in the sea we heard the loud vulgar laugh the two men letting, as soon as they see us coming they turned their mouth.

'What Dolphus telling you dey Mr Alvar? I sure is some stupidness,' Aunt Sarh teased.

'Nutting. Nutting Miss Dolphus. You don't stay long in the sea. What happen Dorothy all of a sudden you 'fraid sea water?'

''Fraid what sea water? Behave yourself nuh Mr Alvar. Me and Aunt Sarh just went for a cool out.'

107

Aunt Sarh sat down on one end of the bench from Uncle Dolphus. I sat on the big stone and leaned against the tree.

'Mr Dolphus was just telling me how some people in England make horse eat their money till they turn imbecile.'

'He don't believe me Sarh. Tell him. Some of them if the betting shop open on Sunday they will be there. Whether in the shop or the race track. If they started cat race these men will back them. They know the names of all the horses not to mention the jockey. They know who leading from who can't ride donkey . . . everything. If you listened to them you will think that's all that was in their head.'

'You used to back horse too. Don't go on as if you never back them. When you used to come by me the first time every Friday and Saturday night you say you going to the dog track.'

'You didn't believe me, did you? You didn't believe me at all. You thought I had another woman. Lord I never meet anybody so jealous in my life. Everytime I tell this lady I going to the dogs with Jim she swell up like bullfrog,' Uncle Dolphus laughed. 'Lord she jealous.'

'Chupes. Who jealous! Jealous for what! I didn't used to take you on. All you man lie too damn much.'

'Don't bother with her eh Mr Alvar. Dorothy, your aunty is the most jealous person I ever meet; believe me. You know how I manage to get her to come to the dogs with me?'

'Here he go again. Dolphus you could bring up some old long time talk eh. And is not even true.'

'What happened Uncle Dolphus? Tell us.'

'You Dorothy worse than Dolphus. You have time to listen to him and his stupidness.'

'What happened Uncle Dolphus? What happened?' I pumped him.

'Lord this woman jealous. All the time I asking her to come

108

with me and Jim she saying dogs track is for man. Gambling is not for woman. She go on like that until I mentioned that Jim girlfriend coming. I don't know what happened in her head. Perhaps she thought if she didn't come with me I will take another woman.'

'Chupes. Dorothy don't bother with your uncle you hear. Mr Alvar is not so the thing go eh. Dolphus always turning things.'

'Haa haa hee hee hee,' Uncle Dolphus laughed. 'Because Jim had his woman outside she thought I might get it in my head too.'

Aunt Sarh shook her head. 'Bunjay all you man is something you know. All you eye long you know. Jim had his wife and children in his house and still go up and down, all in party with another woman. Some of Miss Jim good good friends knew what went on but never opened their mouths. They never breathe a word until Jim died. Until the man dead stone cold and that other woman come pushing up herself was then Miss Jim knew what went on. It was funny how he died though. Really funny.'

'You could say that again; his wife was an old genal. She was only pretending she didn't know Jim had a woman outside. She was only playing innocent. I never understand how this big strong hearty man just lie down in his bed and died. She said all she heard that night was as if he called her name, but she wasn't sure because sometimes he talk in his sleep. Next morning she nudging him to get up to go to work is a dead body that on the bed beside her. Jim dead, dead stone cold dead . . .' Uncle Dolphus voice trailed off.

My blood ran cold when he said that. Imagine you and a person gone to bed good good and getting up to find the person dead. Not a word just dead. Lord!

'Nobody could dead just so. He must had a bad heart man. He heart must be bad.'

'No bad heart Mr Alvar. Doctor said his heart was as strong as any young person. Not that he was old. He only had about forty something,' Aunt Sarh added. 'No bad heart nothing so according to the doctor.'

'So is she kill him then.'

We turned and looked at Mr Alvar. 'Don't look at me so. If nothing wrong with his heart and he went to bed all right it must she kill him. As Mr Dolphus said she must well know about him and that other woman so work something on him. Miss Dolphus you remember once you said that we people go all in England with their nastiness. They hand dirty in their country. They in other people country still they don't wash their hand. Is she kill him so. Is she.' Mr Alvar pressed the idea.

Miss Alma heard us talking under the mango tree she came and joined us. Sometimes I think she don't have anything in her house to do. As soon as she hear Mr Alvar mouth quick quick she coming.

'Who dead? I didn't hear the radio this morning. Who dead?' she repeated.

'Nobody dead. Is England we talking about Miss Alma. Mr Dolphus was just telling us about that friend he had that went to sleep and dead just so. I saying is the wife that killed him,' Mr Alvar informed the other woman.

'Miss Alma, was the same thing people said at the time. They said was she give him thing to drink. All test doctor did they couldn't find anything wrong. They said he died from natural cause.'

'What these doctor and them know eh Miss Dolphus what they know? All they know is bottle medicine.'

'I don't know Mr Alvar. That was very funny but the

110

doctor said he died of natural cause and released the body. Miss Jim buried her husband and little after she picked up her children and went back to St Lucia.'

'Natural cause my foot!' Uncle Dolphus said. 'What natural cause eh? How come he died of natural cause just a month after he win the load of money on the pools eh . . . how he didn't die of natural cause before? I tell you that woman was a genal.'

'He did win money!' Miss Alma was alarmed.

'Yes, he did win a lot of money man . . . aaye aaye. Thousands of pounds he win on the pools. Not everybody knew about it but Jim told me and I told Sarh. He was planning to pack up his work and go back to Guyana. He even told me that he was in two minds. His wife wanted him to go to her people in St Lucia but he wanted to go to Guyana. In the end he said he didn't mind where he went he could make life anywhere.'

'Mr Dolphus you mean he win all that money and in a month he dead . . . all he get from the money was his coffin? Bunjay oye! I never hear that. And doctor say he died from natural cause . . . that funny man really funny.'

'Perhaps was the money that burst his heart you know, could be the money. Perhaps he went to bed thinking about the money and his heart string burst,' Mr Alvar was serious, but we laughed when he said that.

'Yes Mr Alvar,' Miss Alma teased, 'England doctor said the man died from natural cause but you sit down quiet in Grenada years after and know is money that burst his heart string.'

'I still think the wife had something to do with it though,' Uncle Dolphus added. 'Woman too genal. You never know how their minds work.'

Aunt Sarh cut her eyes at her husband. 'More than man. Woman more genal than man eh. All you man eyes too long.

111

If you all stay with one person, the one inside the house there wouldn't be all that trouble. Stick with the person God gave you inside the house.'

When Aunt Sarh said that Miss Alma countenance changed. Sweat drops started peeping out all over her face like sequins on the front of a dress. As for Mr Alvar his face sort of dropped between his legs. He closed his eyes but you see the eye balls rolling about under the skin looking at everybody. Aunt Sarh wasn't really thinking about them when said that, she just said it. Even if she was thinking about what going on between Mr Alvar and Miss Alma she might of still said it. My aunt tongue don't have bone you know, no bone at all. She says exactly what she feels.

'Was about three months after you first went to the Clapton dogs with us he died, ent it Sarh? Was not long after that.'

'No wasn't long at all. I could still see his face laughing at me at the dogs that night.' Aunt Sarh started laughing. She just laughed and laughed. She laughed so much the little plaits on her head were laughing too. 'You remember Dolphus? You remember how the three of you laughed at me?'

'Aaye aaye you think I could forget that? Miss Alma this good lady went to the dog races to try and win some money. She spend the whole evening laughing at the dogs running after the rabbit.'

'Lord I laugh that night for so. I tell you all next day I laughing. Was the funniest thing I take my eyes and see in a long long time. I see some things on the television but I know the people only acting; they only pretending but that was right in front me like you sitting in front me now.' Aunt Sarh eyes was red like loupgarou ah fus she laughing.

Her laughing was catching. Me, Mr Alvar, Miss Alma all of us laughing at Aunt Sarh laughing. Uncle Dolphus laughing at something else.

112

Aunt Sarh filled a glass of passion fruit juice from the little jug on the little table beside the tree and slowly sipped.

'What do those dog and them make she laugh so?' I asked.

'Dorothy,' Uncle Dolphus started again, 'we explained to your aunt about betting on the dog track all right. When the dogs came out on the track we asked her which ones she liked that we would buy for her; that mean put her bet on for her. We explained everything to this good lady. She said she understand, even vex with me because she said I treating her like a child like she don't have any understanding. She so vex she made sure she gave me her own money to buy her tickets although is me that gave . . .'

'I know you gave me the money in the first place you don't have to go telling people,' you should see the eye Aunt Sarh cut at Uncle Dolphus.

'When the dogs started running Sarh burst out laughing. Everybody shouting at the dogs to run faster this lady laughing, laughing long water running down her face.'

'Aye aye how you mean! I laugh oui. You not telling the story good. The thing is they never told me that the dogs not supposed to catch the rabbit.'

'Of course they not supposed to catch it. The electricity will kill them.'

'You all didn't tell me that,' Aunt Sarh and Uncle Dolphus started on each other.

'So what happened?' Mr Alvar asked. 'What happened? Did a dog catch the rabbit that night?'

'Catch what! The thing wasn't real. When the bell ring ding ding Dolphus said to me to look out the rabbit coming. I straining my eyes to see real rabbit. Then I saw this little thing rolling rolling fast fast on the track chuk kur chuck it rolling pass. Then Dolphus said I must look for when the trap door open. As the rabbit passed this box where they had the

113

six dogs pheups the box door fly open, the dogs bolted out and started running behind the rabbit.' Aunt Sarh started laughing again. 'This little rabbit rock and rolling in front and these dogs running to catch it. Running knocking down each other behind that little rabbit. The faster they run was like that gave the rabbit more steam to run. To tell you the truth I don't remember how that race ended ah fus a laughing. That was something that night. That was something. I didn't understand why at least one dog could not catch the rabbit. I thought that it was the one that catch it was the winner.'

Uncle Dolphus shake his head as if even now he can't believe what Aunt Sarh was saying. 'She made of all of us laugh that night. We all had a good night. I think she brought good luck too. All of us win something that night even the woman that came with Jim. All the time she following Jim in the dog track I don't think she ever had any luck.'

'How much you win Aunt Sarh?' I asked.

'I don't remember. I think about £35.00 and some change. I don't remember but I made sure I bought something with the money. That big trunk you see I have in my bedroom was that money I bought it with. That and other bits and pieces.'

'This lady strange for so,' Uncle Dolphus mused. 'She strange. She win that piece of money when I asked her to come with me the next week she quarrelled with me. She started saying she is not a gambler. She don't have time to follow up dog track. She going out with me you know. When she started quarrelling I just went about my business.

'Me! Because I had a little luck the first time you think I was going to make it a habit to follow up dog race. Not me. I went a couple of times later around holiday time but I wasn't making it a habit. I preferred to stay in my house and watch the television. When we lived in St Peter's Street I used to go to the bingo with Mary, that's the same friend I told you about Dorothy.'

'You mean the one that used the man pot that he boiling his dye in?'

'Yes. She self. I used to go to bingo on Essex Road with her but then I find like this place raising my blood pressure too much. You sit down all night waiting for one number; every game you sweating, you sweating, waiting for that one number. Everybody around you calling "house" you sit there sweating. You want fifty-five the caller calling all the number fifties but not fifty-five. You sit there sweating. The heart going boop boop boop ready to jump out of your ears. Every time the caller start a number with five your mouth open ready to shout house, wrong number. To make matters worse the first number in the next game is fifty-five. After a while I stopped going in that place. I couldn't afford to give myself high blood pressure.'

'You didn't want money to burst your heart string nuh. When the heart start going boop boop boop faster than the clock anything could happen.'

'Me, Mr Alvar, not me. When you sit there sweating your nerves start walking all over your body, just walking like you have beast in your skin. Meee saye saye not me.'

11

Me and Aunt Sarh left the men and went to cook the breakfast. They were quiet for a while as if Aunt Sarh talking about her blood pressure made them lose their voices. They seem to forget whatever they were talking about before we joined them. They were quiet then, just as they are quiet now. Sometimes things happen and as if you know it happened before the same same way. Like the way Mr Alvar came down this morning and he still here with Uncle Dolphus is like things repeating itself. As soon as I see the men take the domino board and the rum bottle and went below the tree I knew Mr Alvar not going home before night especially when Mr Joe came and joined them. Sometimes Richard and Ian would join them to knock the domino but since last week I hear they working. Is when these two young men with them you could hear domino language . . . plam pamt platamp knock knock plam domino breaking the table. Sometimes I wonder if is the one that made most noise that win the game. As the domino clapping the table so their throat and the white rum talking. Richard and Ian working and nobody else stayed long enough to play today. Ian don't like working in the road but sometimes you have to turn to anything you could get to make a living, as long as it is honest work. He should listen to some of the things Aunt Sarh does say she had to do in

England to make a living. Like when she didn't want to go out in the cold in the winter to work. Lord I hear somethings about things about this place oui. Aunt Sarh said once she heard people talking about outdoor work so she thought she'll give it a try and if it work out she would not have to go out in the cold every morning. When she talked about outdoor work I stopped grating the coconut and looked at her plum in her face.

'How you mean Aunt Sarh. You don't want to go and work outside the way you always saying how the place cold eh. You did not really go for work outside!'

'Lord, Dorothy when I first hear about this outdoor work was the same same thing I said; these people and them must be crazy. What they were asking for was outdoor machinists. If people mad to work outside.'

'What kind of machine you could use outside in the cold?'

'When they say machine they mean machine you sew clothes with. It was like that woman I told you about in Lonsdale Square who used to work for the Jew man. That's what they mean by outdoor work. You work in your house instead of going to the factory. They bring the work to your house and collect it when you finish.'

'O hoye. I see. So you thought if you get that work it will be better for you!' These people and them could really say some funny things. They saying one thing but mean something else.

'Bunjay; Dorothy it take time to understand some of the things. Anyway when I understand what they wanted I decided to go and ask for work. I had one week holiday where I was working so I decided to try that outdoor work during that week. If I like it and could make as much money as in my job I'll take it.'

'You had a machine?' I don't know what made me ask.

117

'Woye,' Aunt Sarh burst out laughing. 'Woye o yoye. Dorothy I had this little singer hand-machine I used to make my curtain with. To me was a good machine. Anyway I went to this factory and asked for work. I tell you before one of the first thing I learn in England is never to tell these people and them the whole truth. First thing they asked me was if I had any experience.'

All the while we talking Uncle Dolphus sit down on the chair under the window by the dining table quiet quiet like he sleeping. As soon as he hear Aunt Sarh talk about they asked her if she had experience, heum eeeum em, he cleared his throat, pressed his back harder against the wall, twist his mouth as when he ready to laugh but not want anybody to see him laughing. He looking at Aunt Sarh in the corner of his eyes, not straight at all at all.

'So what happened? You got the work?'

'Wait girl, let she tell you. I always say your aunt is something else. This woman is a real genal.'

Aunt Sarh started to laugh. 'It wasn't funny at the time, but I tell you that was something. Well they told me what kind of work it was. It was not hard at all. Then one of the women showed me how to do it.'

'Heeum,' that was from Uncle Dolphus.

Aunt Sarh just twist her mouth at him. 'Dorothy she showed me good good how to put the pieces together, then told me to have a go. I sat down on the little bench bold as brass. Well I told them I had experience ent it. I sit down, that time my bottom jumping like jelly ah fus I nervous. To make bad worse the woman stand up right behind my back watching me. I take my time fix fix the material under the presser foot, take a deep breath and put my foot down on the peddle. Zuuup the needle gone. I jump. You see I never

118

ever used an electric sewing machine in my life. I only had my little bang a rang.'

'Bunjay oye Aunt Sarh suppose the needle did run in your hand. Papa Bunjay look at trouble nuh. What they tell you?'

'When I jump, the woman jump too. Then quick quick she went and call the foreman and tell him I can't do the work.'

'Never mind you did try.'

'Wait, let she finish telling you the story,' Uncle Dolphus butted in. 'The story not finish yet.'

I looked from one to the other. To me after they find out she can't even use the machine they wouldn't give her the work.

'The foreman came over and told me sorry but he understand I can't manage the work. Is because I a bit nervous, especially with the other woman over my head I told him. I get really nervous with strange people that's why I work at home, I told him. I told him if he let me take the work home I could make one or two and bring them back to show him. The work not hard was little children play suit. The trousers to the cowboy and indian set. You should see how the woman swell up when the foreman told her to make up a bundle for me to take home.'

My aunt is something. She is something. 'So you got the work after all.'

'Aye aye how you mean if I get the work; but it didn't last long. I spend the whole evening working and only finished two. It was good. When I brought it back the foreman was really pleased. He gave me a bundle of about fifty to finish by Thursday. That was the Tuesday. When he came Thursday night I only finished about twelve. When the man came in the room and see the hand machine I working on his face colour changed. He said I am a bit slow he wanted people

119

who could work faster. He paid me for those I did and took back the rest. Next week I just went back to my job eh. I tell you you have to try every little thing in England. You have to try . . .' her voice trailed off.

Ian talking about he don't like working in the road is a good thing he have Clarence around him to encourage him. I'm glad that the young men get little work with the government because he could help his mother. Richard get the overseer job while Ian working under Clarence. It better that way because Ian too damn lazy he has to work with somebody who'll be after him all the time otherwise he not doing any work. Another good thing is they not working on this side because if he working in the road and hear the domino knocking he'll sneak away to come and play leaving others to cut his task. I don't know how these men love the dominoes so.

Uncle Dolphus said when he was in England every Saturday night sometimes right to Sunday morning he and his friends used to meet up at each other's house to play. Sometimes they went all the way to a place call New Cross to play. He said they used to really go there to pay the sou sou but they always ended up in a particular pub playing dominoes. He said after a while he stopped following it up so much but other like it was their life. There was another Grenadian man that marriage almost broke up because of the dominoes. From Friday night that man playing. There used to be a kind of club in another friend back basement room. All weekend from Friday to Sunday the men playing dominoes. That Grenadian man wife just had a baby. The woman had three little children to look after, instead of the man stay and help her sometimes he off, and not only that they only had one little room so when he come home late and disturb those children and on top of that she had to go in the kitchen all hours in the night to heat up

120

food for him. All how she talk to him, tell him at least come and have his food early no use. One Sunday she get vex, wrap up the food, put it in a basket, wrap up his pyjamas and his tooth brush and some underwear put it in the basket went to where they were playing and without a word just put every thing down in front of him. Take them out of the basket and plam them in front everybody take she basket and walked out without one word. Not one single word just give him his things and went home to her children. They must get some great pleasure in knocking these things. Uncle Dolphus said it is better down here with the sunshine, cool sea breeze blowing, sometimes if the sea little rough hearing the waves swashing on the shore. It must be different.

Uncle Dolphus and his companion are finished playing for the day, they sat in silence as if pondering, the rum bottle empty, the last piece of ice floating in the bottom of the jug. Mr Alvar leant against the trunk of the mango tree, his cap covering his face. Mr Joe bowcd his head on the domino table.

Uncle Dolphus turned to Devon who had joined them as me and Aunt Sarh left, 'You change the mother goat boy! You give the pig and them some fresh water!'

'Yeh; and I move the donkey over by the pear tree. It have more shade there,' the boy reassured the old man.

The birds swig by. Butterflies float on. The sun rays send silvery streaks on the leaves of the coconut branch. Everything peaceful; everything tranquil. It seemed like time stood still. For how long! It seemed eternity.

Uncle Dolphus gazed across the silvery turquoise water. The cruisers that graced the water in the morning had long gone on their way. The fishing boats had long found their place of occupation. Tiny waves bob up and down as they play with the small fishes that race each other for a glimpse of the shore. Shadows and images dancing, Uncle Dolphus mind their dance floor.

'England, heh England,' Uncle Dolphus mused, 'England.'

'What you say Uncle Dolphus? You talking to me?' Devon perched on a stone looking intensely at his uncle. He seemed to be searching that face for something. 'You want me to go and see if the food ready, eh, you want to see what Aunt Sarh doing? She and Dorothy must soon finish cooking.'

For the instance the old man was oblivious of the child. 'I wonder what Charlie doing. Lord Charlie; that is a man,' he continued to himself.

'Who! Who you talking about?' Devon continued to scrutinise the old man. He adores his uncle.

'Charlie that is a man!' Uncle Dolphus repeated. Mr Alvar and Mr Joe had both dozed off.

'You awright Uncle Dolphus?' Devon was getting more concerned as the old man talked to himself more and more. He could see his uncle's mind was far far away. 'You awright?' he repeated.

'Eh! What you say boy?' The old man looked at the child as if aroused from a trance.

'I ask if you awright.'

Uncle Dolphus laughed, 'I'm all right. I was just thinking about a friend I had in England.'

'You still have plenty friends in England! They does still write you and Aunt Sarh. You does miss them eh. Sometimes you does wish you still in England eh, eh Uncle Dolphus?' Devon's tongue was running away with him as usual.

'Aaye! Sometimes; sometimes. Sometimes I miss the old country but I'm not going back in that cold at all at all. Thank God he spare my life to come and take little sunshine in my bones before he call me. I miss some of my friends yes. If I tell you something you'll think your uncle not right in his head but sometimes I missed the running about. Fancy missing the rat race. Devon in England you always running. It's a rat race country boy. You hear your aunt say she used to run in her sleep is true.'

'You have to run to keep warm eh. When you run you make hot eh.'

The old man laughed, 'Running to keep warm eh. Sometimes sometimes. Most times you just running to live. When I first come home I used to miss going to the pub especially on Friday nights. I missed Charlie for that. Every Friday me and him used to meet up for a few drinks. At first we went to a pub near where we working. Some of the men from the factory used that one as well. When they come in me and Charlie would buy them drinks. We'd have a chat and a laugh. They used to be glad when they came in and see us because they knew we'd buy the drinks. When we in there we buy everybody drinks but I notice when they buying was only for their friends. There was this one in particular called Martin as soon as he put his foot inside the place he would come over and give us big slap on the back. "Hello Adolphus, hello Charlie," and grinning that kind of pork chop grin. He wanted drinks but he never put his hands in his pocket, not for us anyway. Only when his friends came, never for me and Charlie. Not just Martin was the same thing with most of them. After a time me and Charlie stopped going to that pub. That man Charlie was a good friend to me, a good good friend. We used to write each other regularly when I first came but now he stopped. Well perhaps he don't have anybody to do it for him. I used to encourage him to go to night school to learn to read and write. He said he get by all these years he not going and sit down on school bench at his age. I still used to try to get him to go to night school. I tell not all his friends could be friend, when he ask them to read letter for him some of them would not tell him everything in the letter and then go and spread his business. He say he couldn't be bothered.'

'You mean he couldn't read and write? A big man so didn't go to school!' Devon was shocked.

'His parents sent him to school but his head was like dry copra coconut, nothing inside. He said he got vex with a teacher one day and never put his foot back in the school door.'

'How he mean vex with the teacher? You can't vex with teacher and stop go to school.'

'Was not just so. What I remember him saying was that he did something wrong in school and the teacher strap him. He waited in the evening when the man going home hide and stoned him. From that time he never put his foot back in school room.'

'What! You mean he fire stone behind the teacher and his mother and father didn't beat him? Beat him and make him tell the teacher he sorry? If was me my mother would give me one beating I wouldn't have trousers bottom.'

'Devon boy, everybody is not the same. Perhaps Charlie used to box brains on his people the same way he boxing brains in England to make a living. Still he get by. He helped me out when I first went to live in Tottenham. That was before I went to live in Islington where I met Sarh. I tell you something boy those white man and them couldn't play fool with him you know. They had to know their place when they talking to him. Me and him was working in a firm where they make furniture. He used to polish. He was one of the best french polishers in the firm. He been with the firm for about fifteen years, one day a new foreman looked at him and called him boy. Jesus Christ who tell him to do that, eh? Who tell that man to open his mouth and call Charlie Griffith boy.'

'Bunjay oye a big man they calling boy. These people don't have manners nuh. Aaye aaye Mr Alvar you doh hear what Uncle Dolphus say?'

Mr Alvar opened his eyes slightly. At the same time opening his mouth in a wide yawn. Mr Joe mumbled and scratched his leg. There was this thing with Mr Joe and Mr Alvar they always seemed to do things like that together. As if they practised when nobody watching. If one fall asleep the other fall asleep too. When one stretch the other twist. I never see that.

' "Come on boy, move," the foreman shouted again. "I say to leave that and sweep up the locker . . . and hurry."

' "Who you calling boy!?" Charlie measured that foreman face. His eyes squint, his ears squingy, his face changed like when water dripped on ashes and leave water mark. "You find I look like your son."

'The foreman playing bigshot left where he was standing come and poked Charlie on the shoulder, "You boy; you I talking to. Move or . . ." Before he could finish what he was saying, whap wham the piece of chair leg that was by Charlie bench landed across his chest. It happened so fast nobody saw Charlie hand move. It was a few minutes before we realised what happened. That time the foreman hollow out, Charlie grunting ready to land him another lash. I jumped across and grabbed his hand. He was sweating and grunting like an old pig. The other men helped me hold him and try to calm him down otherwise he would killed that foreman that morning. Killed him dead.'

'Good; he should break his head. How he go call a big man so boy and then go and juke him as well? Charlie should of break his hand.'

125

'Charlie dead now Mr Dolphus?' Mr Joe joined the conversation.

'Dead? What you mean dead? Charlie still there. I think he still there. Is a long time I don't hear from him but he must be still there. Charlie not dying now. I could see him now. The front of his head clean clean like that black clean neck fowl Sarh have dey. The front of his head and his forehead all in one. Clean and shining. His two eyes close close together with a little gap to start the nose bridge. When you see he vex you can't see bridge at all. Like the eyes lids squash up with only little straight creases between them. And he shine. Shines just like the mahogany furniture he used to work on. They lost the best polisher they had. He was the best french polisher they had in the factory . . . the best.'

'I mean if he hit the white man they must lock him up. The way I hear about some of these police they could kill him in jail,' Mr Joe commented.

'They didn't lock him up but he lost his job though. He didn't wait for them to sack him. He picked up his things and walked out. The foreman wasn't badly hurt. More his pride that was hurt.'

'Hmm that Charlie lucky then. Not the way I hear how police does pick up people in the road, put in the cell them beat them up for nothing. Hmm, Charlie is a lucky man.'

'Hmm.' Uncle Dolphus lapsed into a faraway trance again. He gazed across the water. Little fishing boats were meandering by. He didn't really see them. The creases in his face like a map. Could be the map of England.

'Dolphus, Dolphus oye come come the food ready,' Aunt Sarh called from the kitchen window. 'Mr Alvar come and get something to eat. Since morning you up here time to get something in your belly before the worms start jumping. Dolphus come come.'

126

'Uncle Dolphus, Aunt Sarh calling you,' Devon gently shook the old man.

Uncle Dolphus roused from his dream. England faded in the distance. He became aware of his wife's voice.

'Sarh you call? Anything to eat yet? The worms in my belly crawling. They hungry.'

'She calling you for the breakfast,' Devon told him again. 'Aunt Sarh say the breakfast ready.'

The men stood up. Mr Joe shook his legs, 'Lord these old bones stiff. As soon as I sit down they stiff up an go to sleep. Sometimes like they don't want to wake up at all.'

'Ha ha ha,' Uncle Dolphus laughed. 'What you talking about foot stiff Mr Joe? What you saying? If you had the old cold in you body as me what you go say. I know sometimes to get out of bed some morning used to be trouble. The whole body stiff . . . the whole whole body. You have to get up in a cold room. Get up to light a heater to warm up the place before you could change your clothes. Fus it cold steam coming out of your nose like it is a hot pot. You open your mouth steam blowing out of your mouth just like you see steam on the road here when the sun hot, but is cold, it cold.'

'You mean you blowing ice man?' Mr Alvar added.

'Eeeh, blowing ice . . . blowing cold wind right down in your belly man right in your belly. Sometimes you get up water freeze up in the kitchen. You can't even get water to boil a pan of water. Kitchen water freeze, toilet water freeze . . . freeze . . . block up.'

The men started walking towards the house. They moved slowly each in their own thoughts. Their faces registered volumes of history books.

'Miss Dolphuuuss oye I coming?' Mr Joe shouted.

'Aye Mr Joe.' Aunt Sarh called back. She knew he only called to remind her that he is coming to eat. Aunt Sarh

127

laughed to herself in the kitchen, 'That Mr Joe eh that man. He making sure I take out food for him.'

'You throw eyes on the mother goat boy. You give the pigs some water?'

'Yeh Uncle Dolphus they awright. I change the donkey too.' The child walked beside the men. He looked at them sideways; from one to the other. He smiled. They walked on in silence. They entered the house through the downstairs steps leading to the dining room.

'Sarh oye. I hungry girl . . . I hungry like . . .'

'Since morning you beating mouth you doh must hungry. Come come the breakfast ready.' While Aunt Sarh was dishing out the food I set the table for the men. Aunt Sarh said the fish Mr Alvar brought this morning was not enough for dinner but then she decided to stretch it. She said instead of cooking the pease soup she cooked some rice and pease because Uncle Dolphus loves his rice and pease. He don't like plain rice at all. He says it gives him wind. Sometimes he makes us laugh. He say plain rice and boiled English potato make him break wind all day like donkey . . . purp purrrupup purp. Sometimes all in the road he breaking wind like motor car backfiring. In England no matter how dear the provision was Aunt Sarh used to buy it to mix the food. Even after all these years away they still like their local food . . . the yam, sweet potatoes, tannia, dasheen, fig and the fresh fish. Especially the fish. Aunt Sarh say in England the fish they calling fresh is about six months' old. Nothing but ice. When the ice thaw out the fish soft soft you could hardly hold it to clean it properly. All how you season it, it don't have taste. Not like home where you get the fish in the bay as soon as the fishermen come in. As soon as we sit down to eat the bus dropped Miss Alma.

'Miss Dolphus I come back,' she called, 'I just come back.'

'Oye Miss Alma, I in the kitchen,' Aunt Sarh put her head

out the kitchen window and answered her neighbour. Lappa started whinging. 'She coming,' Aunt Sarh whispered. Mr Alvar cleared his throat.

'Mr Dolphus you dey. Aye Miss Dolphus you come out in town quick we.'

'I didn't bother go again. I'll ask Cherry to buy the tablets for me tomorrow when she go to work. Was only that I wanted in town really. How you niece?'

'Miss Alma, I didn't know you niece sick again. When she take in?' Mr Alvar asked.

'You mean you niece in Grenville? You sister daughter you tell the wife about last week dey?' Mr Joe enquired. 'I thought she was better now after she come out the hospital. Sometimes these doctor and them say they have big big certificate they don't know more than me and you.'

'It depends on what the sickness is. Is not all sickness doctor medicine could cure you know, not all sickness at all,' Mr Alvar added.

'You could say that again. It have sickness and sickness. I don't think any doctor in hospital could cure my niece. I tell my sister to go and get somebody to bathe the girl. Give the girl a good bathe to wash out the jumbie on her. She saying she don't believe in these things, but the girl well sick. I go up there and my niece hardly know me. She sit down under the big sapodilla tree just wringing her dress tail . . . wringing her dress tail and talking to herself. When for she to go inside she keep saying to tell this man to move from in front door and let her pass. No man in front the door, nobody there at all. In the night is worse. A night in last week she take a sharpen cutlass and started chopping up the mattress saying there is a big serpent on the bed . . . I don't know, I don't know at all . . .' Miss Alma voice trailed off.

'Your sister don't believe in these things but people with

129

dirty hands working them and hurting others. They practising their nastiness quite in England. Quite in this big country they doing their thing what you think of in this little place. We don't all believe in nastiness, but I always say where there is light there is darkness,' Uncle Dolphus added.

12

The food was on the table, stew down fried fish, rice and pease, provision (fig, dasheen and yam), callalloo side dish and passion fruit juice. We started eating. I brought a plate for Miss Alma too. Devon sat on the step leading to downstairs, his hands making contact with his mouth but his eyes and ears glued on the people at the table.

'You mean we people go all in England with their dirtiness?' Mr Joe was curious.

'Aaye what you talking about Mr Joe. All where we go we go with our thing,' Aunt Sarh said.

Mr Alvar laughed. His mouth full of food but he still trying to talk. I wanted to tell him it's bad manners to talk with his mouth full but he should know that.

'If we people going all in England doing their dirtiness why not try working on the white man when they making them see trouble?' Everybody had to laugh.

'Perhaps they trying it out. We don't know,' Uncle Dolphus added.

'Could be in truth you know. Dolphus you remember that woman that went for divorce?'

Uncle Dolphus put down his fork, emptied his mouth and started laughing. 'Bunjay oye I never hear anything like that in my life. The woman sue the husband for divorce. She complained that he ill treating her and she want to finish with him but she want almost all the things they had in the house, the house and the money in the bank. So the man put solicitor on his case because he said he not giving her anything. If is divorce she want he will give her divorce but he not giving her all that he sweat for in England. When people talked to him he said he don't mind giving her something because she worked as well. The woman didn't want that; she wanted everything. She said she want to see him walking England street begging bread.'

'Aye aye she brass oui,' Devon shouted out.

'Devon! Big people talking. Nobody talking to you. Shut you mouth or go downstairs and eat you food,' Aunt Sarh chastised the boy.

'But that was brassness for so. How she could want everything,' Mr Alvar said.

'Em, emmmm,' Miss Alma cleared her throat.

'Wait nuh, all you don't hear nothing yet. The man was a friend of my friend Charlie, that was how I come to know about it. They came from Carriacou, both he and wife. That case went on for a long long time. Registrar can't settle it. It ended up in the Royal Court of Justice. Is when it reached the High Court things really started happening. Every time the case to call something happened. The last time the case started good good. In the High Court in London . . . the highest court in the country you know. It started the Monday morning to finish perhaps Tuesday or Wednesday. Come Tuesday news reach the court house that the judge that trying the case dropped down dead . . . just so. The man went home the evening and dropped down dead.'

Everybody was quiet. Spoons and forks were halfway between plate and mouth. Eyes fixed on Uncle Dolphus.

'Bunjay oye look at my trouble today nuh. What is this I

132

Joseph Pascall hearing dey? Mr Dolphus, you don't mean to tell me that Carriacou woman went quite in the High Court and work obeah on the judge! Lord give me strength.'

'Mr Joe nobody know what happened. We don't know how the judge died. But what everybody said was the Monday morning when they called the case when everybody gone inside the court room and sit down Miss Marshall, that's the wife, wasn't there although all the while she was outside. She was outside sitting by herself. One thing she kept on asking the usher was what number was the court room. When she told her it was court 43 she asked if she could go in another room because she don't like that number. They told her no, because that was how it's been listed. All before the case ready to start she outside as soon as case ready to start she disappeared. All shout the usher shouting her name no Miss Marshall. They said give her a few minutes perhaps she gone to the toilet.'

'She lucky, you know. She lucky they even waited for her. Some other judge will just dismiss the case and make her pay the court for its time and all the husband lawyer fees. When I heard what happened I just shook my head. One day Charlie brought the husband home to see us. They came for Dolphus to go in the pub and they told me about this case. Dolphus already told me what Charlie told him. That was something, we people never change, never.'

'So whey she was all that time?' I wanted to know as much as the others.

'Nobody knew. Nobody found out where she was. When the usher went back outside, Miss Marshall was standing in front the court room door but won't go inside. She asked the usher if the judge is in the court. When the usher told her no, she must be inside before the judge, she said she wanted to see the judge sitting in his chair before she go into the

133

court house. I hear one thing that morning. The poor usher had to go and talk to the court clerk and ask what to do. Anyway they got the judge in. The court clerk went in his room in the back and told him what was going on. He said is all right he will come in. Aye aye the judge sitting in his seat. Miss Marshall peeped inside. Then she decided to come in. Well, Mr Marshall said he never see white people change colour so in his life. When Miss Marshall come inside the court room the place was as quiet as when they cremating a dead body. He looked at the judge, the man face kept changing colour from white white to red then to reddy-white then God knows what colour. The woman coming in the court room humming. Not only that she came in the room backwards. From the door right up to her seat she walked backward. The judge can't see her face. People didn't know if to laugh or what. Even when she going in the box to give her statement she walked backwards.'

'They should lock her up,' Miss Alma commented. 'Fancy going quiet in court house and making macaquee with yourself. No wonder they treat we people so sometimes.'

'Before she start to give evidence she took out a little bottle in her bag and rubbed down her whole face. While she doing that she not looking at anybody. Her head down and the eyes kind of slanting to one side. I hear the woman made one pappyshow with herself in the court house.'

'Perhaps was smelling salts she using. Perhaps she was feeling bad.'

'What smelling salts you talking about Dorothy? You ever see smelling salts could make a whole room smell like doctor shop? I don't know what it was but come half day the judge put back the case for the next morning. He said he wanted to read some papers. By next morning the news came that the man dropped down dead in the night.'

'Heem . . . hmmm, look at trouble, look at trouble,' Miss Alma groaned. 'People didn't think . . .'

'But Mr Dolphus, they can't say is the woman that killed the judge eh?' Mr Joe was serious.

Me! I just started laughing. Just imagine newspapers writing that 'Black woman kill High Court judge by Obeah,' woye oy yoye; that must sell papers in England for so.

'Dorothy you laughing. But the woman could of been in serious trouble. Perhaps the man had a weak heart if it give out just so,' Mr Joe insisted on defending the woman.

'Em eh em that's funny, real funny. How his heart didn't burst any other time, eh? When people hand dirty they hand just dirty. They could do their nastiness anywhere. Look at my niece. Just look at Nelcia. Nice nice young girl, just look at her now.'

'You mixing up things Miss Alma. You just mixing up things. That did not happen to the judge any other time because you could only die once, only once. I agree with Mr Joe, the judge had a bad heart and it just gave way. If they thought Miss Marshall or what she name was had anything to do with the death what you think would of happened to her eh, just imagine?' Aunt Sarh was trying to have the last word on the matter.

'What happened to the case eh Uncle Dolphus? Did the man win?'

'Devon!'

'Sorry, Aunt Sarh. I go hush my mouth.'

'The case never got to court again. Every time the solicitor ask for it to be listed, the people telling him the list full. It went on like that until . . . well, I don't know. The last time Charlie wrote me he said Mr Marshall turn idiot in England. He walking up and down the road talking to himself and begging. Nobody going near him ah fus he smell bad. The

135

old clothes on him is nothing but rags. The man turn a tramp . . . a tramp. After all the work he work in England he turn tramp. Before I left England they did sell the house and the woman went about her business.'

'I always say woman too genal, too too genal. After the man worked so hard in England he ended up a tramp on the street and she get everything for she and she children. I tell you woman, heh woman,' Uncle Dolphus lamented.

'Why you don't eat you food. You going on as if it is all woman fault. You see some people on the street you feel sorry for them but is them that bring destruction on themself, is them. Sometimes is retribution that following them. So don't go blaming all woman.' I tell you, as if Aunt Sarh ready to curse Uncle Dolphus. He just cut his eyes and carry on eating.

When we finished eating I cleared the table while the others sat chatting. A day like that Mr Alvar would spend the whole time by Uncle Dolphus, and now Mr Joe with them, nobody in a hurry to go anyway. Miss Alma as well. She come back from Grenville she don't even go up and see if thief gone with her place. It's nice and relaxing in the dining room. With the windows wide open the breeze from the sea nice and cool. The zaboucca and breadfruit trees shade that part of the house. Uncle Dolphus and Aunt Sarh like it when people spend time with them. It give them a chance to talk about England.

'Dorothy, make up some food for the pigs to have later eh. Leave the wares. Desiree could wash up when she come. Come come and sit down and rest yourself. You always on at me how I always working but you just the same. Always finding something to do. Don't worry, it run in the blood.' Aunt Sarh sat on the easy chair nearest the window. She picked up an old straw hat and fanned herself.

136

'Talking about court house, Dolphus, you remember about the case about that Guyanese woman in the other court house?'

'What working in that brain of yours now eh?' Uncle Dolphus scanned his wife's face. 'What woman you talking about now?'

'You know the one I mean? You remember when my niece was working in the court house in Duncan Terrace in Islington? In England I get to know my brother child. Beryl and them never send to tell me anything about my brother having children until I write and tell them I meet Marcia in England. Not a word. Was by chance I get to know the child. Marcia is such a nice young woman. She had brains too.'

'Aaye Aunt Sarh, Mammy and them didn't want to worry you with how Uncle Kenneth was behaving. Was not the only child he had. He had other children. My uncle didn't care where he put this thing God give him. Marcia mother was fed up with him. She didn't even want the child to have anything to do with the family, that's why she ran away. First she went to Trinidad, then when Uncle Kenneth trace her and threaten to take Marcia away from her she made it to England. To begin with she said the two children was my uncle's but he said Sheila is not his child, only Marcia. When Marcia born Miss Gatta wouldn't even let the child father see her but she wanted maintenance. I hear uncle Kenneth write her one letter. She wouldn't meet him to talk face to face so they had it out in the letter. I don't know how Miss Gatta think she could hide Marcia from the family. The girl look like Tanty Clarita like anything. You see how Tanty Clarita mouth look like she always ready to cuss bad word? Just so Marcia mouth. Mammy said could be because Tanty Clarita didn't like Miss Gatta. From the time she heard what going on between the woman and her brother my aunt vex

vex vex, even ready to make confusion. Marcia didn't only look like Tanty Clarita she used to move like her too sometimes. You didn't find so Aunt Sarh!'

'Is true you know Dorothy. When I come down here and met Clarita was the same thing I said to Sarh. She reminded me of the niece in England. You right, same same mouth.'

'I don't know. I remember Dolphus saying that in truth but I didn't take much notice. I was more thinking that quite in England I meet the girl. If I didn't go by my cousin Anson that day I wouldn't know I had a niece in England and right in London. Was Anson that make me know my brother child.' Aunt Sarh was quiet for a few minutes like she resting her mouth.

'Come to think about it you right you know Dorothy,' she started again. 'Marcia have Clarita mouth bad bad. She was so nice. When she found out me was her aunt she used to treat me good good. Sometimes every other Sunday she'd come and look for us. She and Dolphus used to get on like father and daughter, like they know each other long long time. She was such a nice friendly person.'

'And very clever,' Uncle Dolphus added, 'I used to tease Sarh about how Marcia couldn't be her family because she too clever. She had a big job in the courts, not the High Court but a smaller court. This one they don't try big cases only cases about money and when landlord bring up their tenant in court for rent and things like that. I think I remember the case Sarh talking about. Marcia was laughing so much when she told us we couldn't understand what she was saying.'

'She was laughing so much when she was telling us, imagine when the thing was actually happening. She said she had to leave the court and go outside because she might of lose her job for laughing in court. She used to sit with the judge. Making up his papers and helping him with cases and things

138

like that. Dorothy, you cousin was very clever. She had a good brain on her shoulder.'

'What about the Guyanese woman eh Aunt Sarh? What about her?' I always like to hear about what went on in court house. I never been to listen to cases not even in Gouyave but when people come out I like to listen to them about what went on.

'Your Honour it was not straight . . .' Aunt Sarh started but couldn't say anything else, not anything we could understand anyway ah fus she laughing, laughing and wagging her fingers. Uncle Dolphus looking at her and shaking his head.

'I tell you what happened,' Uncle Dolphus said. 'Was these two women in court . . . a Guyanese woman and a white woman. They were living next door to each other. The white woman brought the other one to court because she say she interfering with her. She told the court she had no peace in her flat. Even when she cleaning in front her door the other woman coming out and provoke her. She told the judge one day she sweeping in front her door when the Guyanese woman came out and jumped on her back.'

'Jump on she back how?' Miss Alma was kind of shocked. 'How you mean she sweeping and the other woman jump on her back? Lie she lie.'

'That's what she told the judge.'

'Nothing could go so. She is horse for the other woman to just jump on her back. Saye saye that woman must be jockey,' Mr Joe added.

'Wait nuh let me tell you all the story. When she said that the Guyanese woman jumped up and ask her to repeat what she said. I hear she could speak real nice. Nice and proper.'

'What they call real speaky spokey,' Aunt Sarh joined in.

'Speaky spokey. What's that Aunt Sarh?'

'Dorothy, I tell you some of we people in England when they

139

ready to cut style with speech even them don't understand what they saying. They swallow up their lips and talking inside their nose you'd think they had operation in their mouth or something. Some of them not only speaky spokey you should see them walk. Especially some of we own Grenadian. When you meet up some of them they walking stiff stiff like they have board back. Their bam high high up in the air like when black ants climbing soursop tree. Heh when you think is style they cutting is constipated some of them constipated. Is mess they want to mess and they can't mess. I tell you sometimes I felt like offering them a good dose of castor oil.'

When Aunt Sarh said that the laugh that broke out if jumbie passing they must run.

'Aye aye all you laughing. Is true. They pretending they cutting style all the time is in latrine they want to go. That Guyanese woman was like that. Not constipated but speaky spokey. I hear she turned to the woman and said, "Deloris did you say I jumped on your back?" "Yes," Deloris answered. "I was sweeping the step, you came out of your flat and jumped on my back." "Deloris," she said, "if I jumped on your back do you think you'd be standing in front the judge now? Do you think you will be able to get up let alone to come before this judge to tell him that I jumped on your back! You will be dead, dead, Deloris!" Marcia said one laughing in that court house, even the judge had to laugh.'

I could just imagine; Aunt Sarh telling us what happened and everybody holding their belly laughing, if we were there it would of been worse.

'Miss Dolphus saying the thing as if she was in the court house,' Mr Alvar mumbled between laughter.

'Me, Mr Alvar I never put my foot inside court in my country you think I going quite in England to end up in court house? I telling you all how Marcia did tell us. Anyway,

140

sometimes you read some of these things in the papers. Other times people who in the court house at the time come out and tell others what happening. Like the time that judge had to go to a hospital to try a case.'

'In a hospital! What he go in the hospital for? If those people and them sick the only judge they want is papa God. These people have too much thing in their skin. You don't think so?' I turned to Miss Alma.

'If they have thing in they skin. They too happy; that's what happen to them, they too happy.'

'I don't know about happy. I think this one gone in the head clean clean. He was in a mental hospital with a big sore foot. First they had him in prison but then he developed that bad foot. I hear that foot bad, so it stink. Nothing they put on it would dry. Instead it getting worse. It get to the stage that doctor decided the only way they could save the man life was to cut off the foot.'

'Lord have mercy. Dey trouble start. But Miss Dolphus if he had bad foot how come he end up in mental hospital?'

'I don't know Mr Joe, I don't know. I tell you sometimes these doctor and them doing what they want with you. Throw you in mad house and say under section this that and the other you mad and they have the power to do what they want with you. Only power I believe in is the power of God. Could be what happened to that man, I don't know. What we hear was the man went in jail serving something like seven years for whatever after about ten years he still in the place but ended up in the jail hospital because they say apart from the big sore foot he mad.'

'So what that had to do with the judge? I doh see that anything to with a big judge.'

'You think you does hear anything in Grenada or in the whole Caribbean; you think you does hear anything? You

141

think judge in the court house in town go take himself and go quite in hospital to try case because the person mad. They good dey.'

'Chupes. You said was something to do with doctor chopping out his foot.'

'Yes he had that bad foot and doctor want to chop it out to save his life. The man said nobody cutting off his foot. He prefer to died before he let anybody cut off his foot. If God wanted him to have one leg when he born he would of given him one leg. When I heard that I said if he want to dead with his sore foot why they don't let him go?'

'Aye aaye the man right. You don't think so Miss Dolphus? He born with his two foot. If he don't want to cut it out I don't know what that have to do with any judge. I never hear that yet.'

'I still don't understand what that had to do with the judge. If he in hospital he don't do any crime. His foot is his foot. He don't want them to cut if off even to save his life what that have to do with judge,' Mr Alvar was in the dark just like us.

'What happen! The judge didn't really go in the hospital nuh?'

'How you mean he didn't go? Is all part of the system,' Uncle Dolphus tried to explain. 'Some of the doctors said he mad, he don't know what he saying, but one top doctor said the man had all his senses. He knows exactly what he saying. Sometimes he drift a little but most times he all right. That's why they decided to call the judge. Everything had to be done according to the law.'

'Law and I hear some of them so wicked. According to what I hear some of them scamp and them using the law like children using their mother petticoat. Anyway what happened. The judge made them cut out the foot because it

142

smell too bad. Lord that hospital ward must smell like . . .' Mr Joe tightened his mouth and jawbone as if somebody interfered with him.

'Lord that place must smell bad in truth.'

'Yes, Desiree; you know how it smell. You always dey to put you mouth when you hear people talking,' Devon cut across his cousin.

'They take out the judge in London, bring him miles, miles to that hospital to try the case because they say that man too sick to travel.'

'Poor judge.'

'Poor judge what; he working his money. The only thing I wonder is if he went in the hospital wearing the big black robe and white wig that they usually wear. Fancy going into a mental hospital dressed like that . . . all in black with a big long black cloak and white wig. The patients and them must think is another patient that come to join them. Heh, he agreed with man though. He said if the sick man don't want his foot cut off doctor had no right to amputate it.'

'That might be good and bad at the same time,' Miss Alma added. 'What happened to him, he dead?'

'We don't know. We never heard,' Aunt Sarh plamp her hand over her mouth as if to say end of story.

'The person that did tell us about it had a daughter working in the High Court at the time. After the case you don't hear what happened to people,' Uncle Dolphus added. 'Just like down here things hot hot for a few days then you don't hear anything again. Like when that man went and sit down on the Queen bed.'

'What!' Mr Alvar shriek.

'Lord my brain funny oui. I don't know what make me remember that now. Sometimes we talking and all kind of different things coming up in the head.'

143

'What you mean man sit down on the Queen bed Uncle Dolphus?' I turned to look at my uncle. 'Whey that man come out?'

'You doh mean in Buckingham Palace where she and the Prince living nuh?' Christine turned back on her way to the kitchen.

'How he get in that big place? You ever go and see Buckingham Palace Uncle Dolphus? Eh you ever go and see the Queen? The Palace must be nice and pretty. I'll like to go in England boy to see Buckingham Palace, the Queen, to walk in the snow, to watch television . . .'

'Aaye, aye. Devon why you don't ask your mother to send you in England for snow to bite you skin? Every minute you on about England England. I don't know why you don't go for snow and that smoky thing to full you brains.'

'Desiree, leave me alone eh leave me alone. Is my mouth if I want to talk. Just leave me. The Queen house must be big and pretty. You ever see it Aunt Sarh?' Devon repeated, turning to Aunt Sarh.

'If the place big. Me and Dolphus went to see it about twice. I liked to see the guards and them marching up and down in front the gate keeping guard, but I find the Palace itself could do with a good painting up. Even the net curtains in the window could do with a good washing and bleaching. They grey grey like the room always full of smoke.

'You never go inside?'

When Desiree said that Uncle Dolphus started one piece of laughing, laughing and pounding the banister boaw boaw boaw like when carpenter working. He laughing started Aunt Sarh off.

'You see you that Dolphus? You see how you eyes making yip yip yip? That brain of yours start something here today

144

you know,' she teased her husband. 'I don't know how these things and them does come in you head.'

'You saying me what's about you eh, what's about you? How come you know what inside my head? Even inside my head I don't have secret from you,' they were both laughing as if enjoying a private joke while we all looking from one to the other, waiting.

'Desiree girl these guards walking up and down in front the gate day and night. Others all around the yard. Police watching everybody and everything. Ordinary people can't go inside this place,' Uncle Dolphus started again.

'Chupes all the watch they watching, Michael what's his name still passed all of them and ended up inside the Queen bedroom,' Aunt Sarh stopped laughing long enough for us to tell us a little piece of the story.

'He went and thief! If police all about how he get inside? They forget to lock the door?'

'Bunjay Devon you is lawyer. Boy how you could ask question so.'

'Cousin Dorothy I just find it strange that police all about and the man still get inside that big place.'

'Saye saye oye that was a thing the morning they catch him oui. Radio bawling, television bawling, newspapers headline jumping at you. All of them one thing, "Man found sitting on the Queen's bed." '

'Wait nuh Miss Dolphus that's wasn't true though. I mean they were joking eh, just making joke? In the first place I think that a person must be crazy to do such a thing. The other thing you say police all about. I sure they have gun to shoot down people. How they didn't see him? Nuh that must be a joke.'

'Wasn't a joke, Mr Joe. Not a joke at all. Tell him Dolphus, tell them.'

145

'Joke; that was no joke. Michael what's-his-name break into Buckingham Palace, found the Queen bedroom, had the cheek to go and sit down on the bed and started talking to her. Was early early in the morning.'

'The poor woman must be frightened. She must be wet herself in that bed.' I was thinking if something like that happened to me I would mess myself.

'Lawd my head,' Miss Alma squeezed her temples. 'What I this girl hearing dey. The man wasn't right in the head Miss Dolphus. He had to be either crazy or drunk. He wasn't good at all. Go inside the lady room and sit on her bed. Lawd.'

'Whey she husband? He sleeping so hard he don't hear somebody in his room? He sleeping until he dreaming, people could come and do his wife anything and he don't know eh. What kind of husband is that? Chupes,' Mr Joe vex.

'Perhaps he went to work early.'

'Perhaps he just got up and went to the latrine or something.'

'I think he went and make some tea. I hear English people love their cup of tea first thing in the morning. If the house so big the kitchen must be far from the bedroom so he couldn't hear the man.'

'Bunjay look at the poor lady trouble nuh. She must of been 'fraid for so. What he telling her that time of the morning eh.'

Everybody putting in their own opinion of what happened that morning.

'If was me eh, I tell you if was me,' Mr Joe got up, pushed up his shirt sleeve, rolled his fist as if he ready to fight. 'If was me I would give that man one beating. Damn farse. If is woman he after why . . .'

'But Mr Joe we talking about the Queen you know . . . the Queen of England. Aye aye not any and anybody, the big Queen,' Miss Alma emphasise. 'When these people and them come down here you don't see how nobody could get close to them. Even when they shaking hands they always have on long long gloves.'

'Perhaps they have fennae hand that's why they have to wear gloves even when the sun splitting earth.'

I cast eyes at Christine. 'Chupes,' my lip just jumped out with the chupes because I don't understand all that. Not what Christine said about the fennae hand but if the house so big how the man know where the Queen bedroom was?

'She husband must be imbecile or something. If was my wife this man cross his bounds with the beating I would put in his skin only papa God alone would be able to help him, heh I'd put one beating in his skin,' Mr Joe emphasise.

'But Aunt Sarh, Uncle Dolphus where was Mr Prince. I mean the Queen husband?' Desiree asked again. 'If that happened early in the morning? These people and them don't go to work. Whey he was?'

'Heh perhaps he didn't sleep home that night. He don't have to tell people his business. Perhaps sometimes he sleep out,' Miss Alma said, adding, 'all man is man.'

'Kroom koom koom,' Aunt Sarh started to cough. Coughing as when you spit choking you. The same time I glanced at Mr Alvar. He trying not to look at Miss Alma.

'These people and them funny. Me; you think I have my wife she sleeping in one room and me in another room? What I have my wife for then eh?' Uncle Dolphus said that in a kind of way as if he was more talking to himself.

Mr Joe face went up 'juuup'. You could feel his eyes boring into Uncle Dolphus head. 'What you saying man? You doh saying the Queen and she husband don't sleep in the same bed and you always saying the place cold like like hell? What is this I hearing?'

Plap play clap a plap, Miss Alma jump up, start walking up

147

and down the verandah clapping her hands. 'Woye o yoye what I hearing. Because the woman is Queen she husband can't sleep on the same bed with her? Well since I born I never hear that yet.'

'Perhaps she was not well and Mr Prince snore in the night. Could be that. Perhaps she had a bad cold.' Only Devon could think of that.

'I don't know the people business. All I know I making sure my wife is next to me when I go to sleep in the night. And God help the person that farse enough to break in there to interfere with her. The place cold like hell me in one bed my wife . . .' Uncle Dolphus started muttering to himself again.

'So what they do with that man?'

'They arrest him and lock him up. I don't remember how the case pass. You remember Dolphus? You remember how the case pass?'

'They put him in jail. I doh remember what time he get.'

'Put him in jail he lucky. He lucky is only jail he get. Somewhere else his family had to go and claim the body. The way I hear the police does beat up people he lucky he only end up in jail. The man damn farse man, he damn out of order, aaye aye,' Mr Joe vex you'll think was his family or even somebody he know.

Everybody was quiet as if secretly planning their own punishment. As if everybody forget what Aunt Sarh was telling us before Uncle Dolphus remembered about the man on the Queen bed. I didn't forget. Was not the first time they start one story and end on something completely different. Uncle Dolphus said he think he had more than one brain and sometimes they fight to tell story first.

'Aye aye Aunt Sarh you was telling us about that Guyanese woman. What's about the finger? You telling us about those

148

two women in court and you shaking your finger and killing yourself laughing.

'Give me a chance nuh girl. Give me a chance and I'll tell you. Wait a minute let me think. Eh heh yes after she said about if she jumped on the other woman back she would be dead she started telling the judge what happened. He told her to wait she will have her chance to tell her story when the witness in the box is finished. She didn't want to hear that. "But your honour she is lying. If I jumped on her back she would be dead . . . dead. You all don't understand. Deloris is lying." The Guyanese woman insisted on giving her evidence. Somehow the judge managed to shut her up and the other woman finished her evidence.'

Sometimes Aunt Sarh telling story as if she was there, you know. She telling you the thing straight straight. Sometimes with all the actions as well. She tell a little then take a little breath like now.

She sipped her drink then started again, 'When the Guyanese woman went in the box she started. Started in her nice cut lip speaky spokey voice. Like the Jamaicans would say the way she carried herself you could see she had some broughtupsee. She turned to the judge and said, "It was six o'clock in the morning when I heard the noise. Yes, your honour six o'clock in the morning. Outside was still dark. I pulled aside the curtain, you know the nice white lace curtain I bought in that new shop on Wood Green High Road, well that time of the morning I pulled it aside a little and peeped outside and I saw it. Your honour I couldn't believe my eyes. When I heard the noise and looked of the window I saw my dog. I saw my little dog I had since she was a puppy. When I saw her the blood rushed to my head. My hands and feet went hot and cold and then cold and hot at the same time. That time my body freezing cold. Your honour I tell you my

149

dog was running along the corridor with flames blazing out of her bottom." '

'What! Fire in the dog bam! What is dis I hearing dey?' Devon had crept on the step playing with Bingo. 'Fire in the dog bam Aunt Sarh?'

Well, everybody was holding their belly. Boaw doaw booaw Mr Joe take over the carpenter work from Uncle Dolphus. I looked at my aunt. Her face like those a nice fresh ripe julie mango. Water was pouring from her eyes, down her cheek, mixing up with the sweat was like she put her head under the pipe.

'You don't hear the best part yet,' she continued after drying out her face. "Yes, you honour," she said. "The dog was screaming and running down the corridor with fire blazing out of its bottom." '

When she saying that you should see how she shaking her bottom. My aunt is something else. I don't know how she is not an actress.

' "Not just that. When I looked out in the garden this woman," pointing to the white woman, "this woman and all the neighbours were there digging. They had forks and things and were digging in the garden. They were digging a deep deep hole." ' Aunt Sarh was trying to tell the story but she had to stop every few minutes. I never see Mr Joe laugh so since I know him.

'Bunjay oye, look at my trouble here today nuh. What do these people and them in England. I tell you when too much snow get inside these people and them head it turned them bazoodee, man. Turn them real bazoodee,' Mr Alvar put in.

'So Aunt Sarh why they digging that hole? Was to bury the dog?'

'Bury what dog Dorothy? This woman went on, "Your honour, I take my eyes and see them dig the hole six feet

150

deep and you know what! You would not believe me, but I take my two eyes and see it. I thought they were digging my grave. Yes that's what I thought your honour. I thought they were digging my grave. I pulled the curtain watching them. You know what they were burying? A worm. I see them burying a worm your honour. Believe me I saw them. They were burying a worm. It was straight like that. Straight like that your honour not going like that." ' Aunt Sarh started wiggling. The finger wiggling and bottom wagging like when dog wagging its tail. 'Marcia said that's when she left the room and went outside. I tell you I never forget that story. She said if she didn't leave the courtroom she would of forgotten herself and laugh in court and she could of lose her job.'

'In England I see something you know. See and hear. Some of the things that happen if you tell other people they'll say is lie you lying.' Uncle Dolphus brushed his face and tightened his jaw. 'They'll think is lie you lying.'

'This woman was mad though Uncle Dolphus. Something had to be wrong with her in her head to go and tell the judge she see dog with fire in its bam and things like that. She must be crazy.'

'She wasn't all that right in the head Devon. As the English people would say, she had a screw loose up there. She used to work in the mental hospital. Hold big big position, next thing she get just like the people she was looking after. It's really sad to see how some people change,' Aunt Sarh put on her serious face. 'Emmn, real sad.'

Everybody was quiet for a while. I was thinking although we all laughed yet it's very very sad. Sad how people could change just like that. One minute you all right, the next you just change.

13

This time of the day the sun was hitting the bottom part of the house. The verandah was cooler, cool and relaxing. Everyone seemed to have dozed off like we went off in a dream.

Peep peep peep. 'Mr Dolphus, Miss Dolphus oye,' the sound shook me up. 'One more time,' pull up in the gap and Hensley calling.

'Aye Hensley what noise you making in the place dey so eh. You think you in the foreroad?'

'Come girl I have something for your aunt. Miss Effie send that for her.'

'Boy you don't have no manners. A big woman like me you calling girl. You don't have manners.'

'Henslaay,' Aunt Sarh opened her eyes. 'You and Dorothy don't tired. All you carry on as two children. I don't know why you two don't married and done.'

'Aye aye Miss Dolphus, Dorothy don't want me. She say I too poor,' Hensley answered from the gap.

'Chupes. You always with you stupidness. Give me the thing eh the passengers waiting,' I took the little bag from the conductor's hand and passed it to Aunt Sarh.

'Thanks. Tell Miss Effie thanks for me. Tomorrow when you going down I'll see what I find to send for her. The clean neck fowl started laying I'll send her some eggs. I don't think her fowl start laying yet. Dorothy remind me when the Rhode Island hatch a chicken is for Elsa and one for Miss Effie grand daugther.

'Aye aye you giving Elsa chicken again? Everytime you give the girl chicken mongoose going with it. The child don't have luck at all. Leave it up here I go look after it for her. When she come up she could look after it for herself. You spoil that child I have deh you know Aunt Sarh? You well spoil her too much. Netta saying you don't give her children anything. Every little thing is my child that getting it. Give Pappajoe the chicken perhaps he will look after it.'

'What Netta talking about? She lazy as louse. She does help me do anything eh; so she lazy so she children lazy. Is you that dey here with me. She expect me to leave you and you child out to give her what I have. Tell you sister to behave herself.'

Aunt Sarh was vex because I mentioned my sister. The truth is they never got on. Even when Aunt Sarh was in England and didn't even known us properly was me she liked. Since she came home is the same thing. At first Netta used to come around all the time but she lazy and she children just like her. As long as you could give them something is all right but as soon as you ask for a little help is something else. Is my older sister but I talking the truth so she lazy so she red eye.

'The sun going down but Lord it make hot!' Aunt Sarh fanned herself with an old straw hat. 'Lord it hot,' she repeated. 'Dorothy, go inside and see what in the fridge to drink. There is the last bottle of lime juice bring it for Dolphus and see what you find for us.' She continue fanning herself.

Uncle Dolphus stirred. Miss Alma got up, brushed her

153

hand across her bottom. Took up her bag and started going down the step. Bingo growled as she stepped over him.

Miss Dolphus I go see you eh,' she turned towards Aunt Sarh. 'Aye aye Miss Dolphus eyes half close and she laughing. You must be having a good dream. They say people does dream even when they not sleeping, you know.'

I looked at Miss Alma. As she talking about dreaming I remembered a dream I had the other night. I dreamt I was in this strange place. I don't know how I got there or what I was doing there. There was a big crowd of people. We were on a river bank. It looked like Grand Roy River. We were looking across to the other side. The houses on the other side were not like the ones on our side. It was so strange the way everyone was just staring across the river as if we were in a dream. You know was like a dream inside a dream. That time the sun splitting earth. Then we noticed pieces of fluffy white things falling on the other side and then when the little breeze blow they started flying on our side of the river. At first we thought somebody was burning corn land on the other side but then we realised the bits of fluff were falling straight from the sky and kind of cold. It felt funny funny. The place hot hot then these cold things like light pieces of shave ice but light like cotton wool started falling. When we looked where the river was, the river was gone . . . disappeared. I don't know how the dream ended but I remembered people praying and everybody come in one. One man started shouting that it is the end of the world . . . the words of the Bible must be fulfilled . . . this is signs and wonders. In the dream I told Uncle Dolphus and Aunt Sarh about the dream. Aunt Sarh asked me if I'm sure I was sleeping, if was not something I hear Uncle Dolphus talked about. I was sure I was in my bed and was a dream. Uncle Dolphus laughed. 'That sounds like snow girl,' he said. 'Was snow all right.

154

Imagine snow falling in Grenada. Snowflake in the sun Sarh. I tell you what, as soon as snow start to fall in Grenada I moving to Africa.' I must wake up then because I can't remember anything else. Just Uncle Dolphus saying he moving to Africa. I looked at Miss Alma and then at Aunt Sarh. Could be true what Miss Alma say about people dreaming with their eyes open but I sure was dream I dream about the snow falling in Grenada. This world is a funny funny world . . . people brains is a funny thing.

'I not sleeping. I just shut my eyes a little,' Aunt Sarh answered. 'I just thinking about the weather in England now. Look how we sit down here bawling how it make hot in the middle of January. In England this time it cold for so. Cold. You outside you cold, you inside you cold. The amount of clothes you have on you, you could sell, the cold still reaching your blood. You have to run run to keep warm. Mind you in that place you always running you know. You get up in the morning is run you running to get to work. To come home is the same thing. Sometimes I think I used to run in my sleep to survive not only to keep warm. There were times my fingers cold until they stiff that I couldn't even open the purse to pay the fares. I had to give the conductor the purse to take out the money. The fingers cold until the burning . . . burning and biting at the same time.'

I went to the kitchen for the drinks. The men began to stir.

'Dorothy look in the cellar and bring a bottle and some ice for me. Mr Alvar and Mr Joe taking a shot before they go home. Bring a bottle Dorothy. Mr Alvar can't go home dry so,' Uncle Dolphus called out to me.

'Lord Dolphus all you don't tired with this rum in this hot sun. I don't know how all you could drink this thing so. In

England you had to have a little drink to warm your blood but . . .'

'Sarh you worry too much. In England was a different thing. We couldn't sit down outside to drink,' Uncle Dolphus teased his wife. 'You have to sit down on top the heater with the glass of rum in your hand and you still cold. Mr Joe, Miss Alma this time so when it make cold you not catching Sarh outside easily. If Sarh not going to work or to do her shopping you not catching her outside.'

'Me! What I put outside. Not only how it cold early early outside dark like midnight. You going to work in the morning it make dark, you coming home it dark. Sometimes only on Saturday and Sunday you could see light inside where you living. It not only cold and dark sometimes the ground slippery slippery. You can't see anything on the ground but as soon as you put down your foot, sluuup, is on you back you end up. There was something they called black ice on the ground. You can't see it but it dangerous for so. Then again there is the fog. You walking in the road you can't see in front you. Like you walking in smoke, thick thick smoke. Me; once God help me to get inside I just sit and watch the television.'

'Television! You used to watch plenty television?' Devon returned from what he was doing. 'I wish I had a television. I could watch John Wayne and all those cowboys and them. You used to watch John Wayne on the television Aunt Sarh?'

'Your aunty didn't like anything with guns,' Uncle Dolphus said. 'I used to tell her was only pretending they pretending but according to her when then come off the television they could do the same thing to people in the street. And another thing, when wicked people see these things on the television they see you in the street and want to practise on you.'

'I right you know. Some people so wicked as soon as they

see these things on the television poor you walking the road going about your business, you don't tell them their eyes black or white next thing you know they ready to beat you up. Just so they ready to fight you and stab you up for nothing.'

'Bunjaye, Miss Dolphus what kind of world we living in, eh what kind of world? Sometimes right here they want to practise these stupidness. But the police and them does wait for them. Let them catch anybody interfering with others, especially old people, heh let the police catch them,' Mr Alvar wiped his face with his handkerchief.

'Down here police protecting the old people, well some of them anyway. But in England sometimes you 'fraid to call police 'fraid to call them if you in trouble,' Aunt Sarh added.

'You telling me. Things getting so bad people 'fraid to call police. You ever hear that?' Uncle Dolphus take up the story. 'The police and dem don't only pick you up in the road sometimes you quite inside you house minding your business they coming. When they going in people house they go in van load. Not one or two cars you know, whole whole van load. Sarh, you remember what happened to that woman down by Brixton side?'

'What happened Uncle Dolphus? The police and them does beat women too?' Devon, curious as ever.

'Beat women. This poor woman inside her house now she cripple for life. They went in her house say they looking for her son. Boaw boaw doaw, they batter down the woman door. When the woman open the door she frightened to see so many police in front the door so early in the morning. She turned and ran up the stairs because she 'fraid. Bang bang bang, they shoot her . . . shoot her in the back.'

'Lawd have mercy,' Mr Joe bawled out. 'Mr Dolphus, you mean just so they shoot the woman? You ever hear they does shoot people in the back? Not even thief they does shoot in the back. Lawd they have something to answer. They have something to tell God when he call their name on the register.'

'She dead, eh Mr Dolphus, she dead?' Miss Alma sort of shouted back from where she was halfway up the steps to the road.

'Papa Bunjay oye what is this I hearing? The police and them must be drunk or something to shoot somebody, a innocent person inside their house, and in the back,' Mr Joe added. 'She dead Mr Dolphus, she must dead?'

'Mr Alvar, Miss Alma, was one thing that time. One thing in the place. They shoot the woman and turn her cripple. Strong healthy woman, working to mind her children end up in wheelchair . . . strong strong healthy woman end up a cripple. The son they looking for not even in the house. The woman don't even know where the boy living, eh, heh,' Aunt Sarh reflected.

'You mean the bullet didn't kill her? She alive after the bullet hit her? She must be strong boy, really strong,' Devon added. And she lucky too.

'Yes, she lucky. That other woman was not so lucky she ended up six feet under the snow . . . dead. They said she had heart attack. Heart attack when they tried to calm her down. Quite inside the woman house you know.'

'They should lock up the police that fired the gun,' Devon face was serious. Uncle Dolphus just looked at the child. Looked at him as if he wanted to say something then changed his mind.

'Aye aye, Mr Dolphus, they make it a habit going inside people house and interfere with them?'

'Mr Joe I tell you these times I 'fraid, 'fraid to go outside, 'fraid to stay inside the house on my own. I used to stand by the window peeping outside until I hear Dolphus key turn in the lock.

158

'What you 'fraid Miss Dolphus? You 'fraid police come in your house too? Bunjay I never hear that in my life. Like you always living in fear. And you all stay in that place so long. The weather one thing but if you living in fear of people and the ones who suppose to protect you, I don't know how people stay in this place at all. So what happened about the woman?'

'Chile was a time in England. After the woman died people started marching and saying enough is enough. Was then the police get bad. They didn't expect black people to open their mouths to say what was happening was wrong. Well they were in for a big surprise. One bacanal in the place. One thing break in the place where the woman died, one fighting. What really made the police get bad was that one of them got killed. Lord Jesus Christ was then thing got bad. They wanted to jail every black person in England for the death of that policeman.'

'Bunjay, Lord I see thing in England you know,' Uncle Dolphus took up the story. 'I see thing oui. Police started raiding everywhere where plenty black people lived. Left right and centre they raiding homes, stopping people in the street anywhere . . . searching you. One weekend every thing shut down. Shopkeepers boarded up their shops because those damn thieves and troublemakers, you know those that only living for making trouble, just waiting for a little breeze to blow to make their move, giving others more bad names, well shopkeepers boarded up their shops to prevent these people and them from mashing up the place and thiefing their goods because groups of people were planning to march all over London – demonstration in front police stations, outside the Prime Minister house, all over the place. Well that weekend the whole place like the burial ground the night before All Saints'. That was one time I didn't put my foot outside. I

159

helped Sarh with the shopping the Friday night and didn't put my foot outside till Monday morning when I ready to go to work.'

'It sound like the time this man came from Trinidad saying that the world ending that Sunday evening. Aunt Sarh you did hear about that!'

This boy could really talk stupidness. Sometimes I could just hit him. 'Devon, shut you mouth,' I shouted. 'You always talking stupidness. You hear police shooting and killing people you talking as priest, well he said he was a priest. The man came over saying he had a visit from God and God tell him to go and spread the word. Tell people to prepare themselves the end of the world is here.'

'Chupes this man was a damn scamp,' Mr Joe added. 'He made people sell all their things and bring the money to him. Kept them in church all that Sunday praying. Devon is right that Sunday everywhere was quiet. I think people in the church didn't want to pray loud in case they don't hear when God came for his world. All the time people lock up in church all over Grenada, not only Grenada but the whole West Indies the man on plane going to America. America you know. Perhaps America is not part of the world. Lord people stupid. The man come and turned every body head. All the while he had his thing well planned with others in the other islands . . . big burburl . . . big big burburl going on. You remember that time Miss Alma . . . you remember?'

'Aaaye I remember oui. Not in St Vincent they catch up with the damn scamp. The plane he was on stop over in St Vincent to pick up people for Barbados on the way to America. I hear they beat him, they beat him. He ended in hospital . . . the damn thief. Thief the people things to go and live life in America. Instead of God coming he almost went to meet God. That is if God had anything to do with him.'

160

'Everywhere had their thing . . . everywhere you go. But that time in England was frightening. Things like that made me wanted more to come back home. Everyday Sarh talking about home, making sure I don't change my mind. I know some people saying they going back to their country and when time come they say they don't think that after all these years in England they could settle down in the sun again. Some even bawling how the sun too hot they can't stand it. God didn't make our body for snow they come bawling they can't stand the sun. Crazy, they crazy.'

'Like that Jamaican woman that married to the Tobago man. You remember them Dolphus? They had a house right in the bottom of St Peter's Street next door to the pub. The man say he tired, the old body want rest. He said he just waiting for the little pension to go back in the sun to rest himself. He didn't mind if is in Tobago or Jamaica. The wife put her foot down saying she not leaving England. She not going one place because she go miss the life. What life she had I don't know. She seeing more trouble than anything else. She worked in the hospital seven days a week from eight in the morning till six in the evening then go and do cleaning in a factory for two hours, hiding every penny she worked for, saying when she dead is for her son. They only had one son and he was a damn vaeneag. He not knocking stroke for a living. He used to make the parents especially the mother see hell. The boy used to tell her to her face he can't wait for her to die for him to get the money. All she did was work and hide the money, work and hide the money. She won't even go on a little holiday, take a little enjoyment, nothing. She didn't even used to feed the body, buy little tonic and thing to drink. I hear once she wasn't well when a friend of hers told her to buy little seamoss and linseed, boil it up and sometimes mix it up with a pint of Guinness to give the

161

nerves a little food, she curse the friend. Tell her she too
damn facetey, why she don't mind her own wawarit business.
The thing was she find she will have to spend a little money
to buy those things. All she did was go to work, go to the
market and sit down home and watch the television. I don't
know what kind of life she talking about she can't leave to
go back to her country. The last thing I heard was that the
man died and she catching hell under the boy. I saying boy is
a big man. When the father died he made the mother sell
her house and give him the money together with the father
insurance money. He told her he buying house for both of
them. The woman so stupid I hear she moved in the house
the boy bought and still had to pay rent for the little room
he put her in in the attic. She had rheumatism in the knees
bad bad. To climb up those four flights of stairs was a problem.
She couldn't even open her mouth to say anything to the son
because he tell her if she don't stop moaning he will throw
her out. When she stopped work was the DHSS that had to
pay her rent and even then he threatening to put to her in
an old people home because he didn't want these people and
them in his house. I think he used to dip his hands in nastiness.
He didn't used to work but he had the best clothes the latest
fashion and things like that. I hear in some of these homes
where he wanted to put the mother they used to beat those
poor old people; they does make them see trouble. And the
boy want to put his mother there after all these years she
work in England.'

'Why she didn't go back to she country, Aunt Sarh? If the
husband died and she stopped work why she don't go back
home? She don't have nobody to go back to in her country?'

'Go back where! How she'll go back? All the while for she
to make preparation she saying she not leaving England. Now
even if she changed her mind she won't go back where she

162

come from or to Tobago she too shame. Perhaps she didn't even used to write her family. She must shame to go back there now. Me! Me Sarah Powell, you think I could ever take another man country for mines and forget where I born? I want to die on my piece of rock. If it was possible I wouldn't mind if when I close my eyes you all rest my bones under the coconut tree where mama bury my navel string. You think I go sit down in England to watch television?'

14

Miss Alma went home. I bet if she hear Mr Alvar still here when it make dark she coming back. The woman bold as brass, sometimes when Mr Alvar sit down beating mouth with Uncle Dolphus and it make dark she coming and sit down then she pretending she 'fraid to go in she house only to ask Mr Alvar to walk with her. Only over the road you know. She does be out all hours in the night she don't 'fraid only when Mr Alvar by us. One night Aunt Sarh do for her. I tell you my aunt tongue don't have bone. As Miss Alma call Mr Alvar to walk with her Aunt Sarh tell him that Miss Mabel home sick he must remember she want her head rub with some limacol. Nothing wrong with Miss Mabel you know, nothing. It was dark you couldn't see Miss Alma face but you could feel how her mouth went beuoop as it swell hard hard.

I brought the drinks. Everybody was now wide awake. As Miss Alma left Desiree came down the steps into the yard, said howdy and sat down.

'Devon, Tanty Mae say to come down,' she turned her cousin. 'She say as soon as you finish you work to come down.'

'Chupes, Desiree you lie too much. My mother not home yet, you too lie she not calling me.'

'Bunjay what do you these two children? How all you could quarrel so? As soon as Desiree come she and Devon start quarrelling.'

'Aunt Sarh you see is not me that start it. Is that Desiree. She think if I go home she go get all the food.'

'You and Desiree always,' I said. 'Desiree know her food in the kitchen.'

'Tanty not calling me at all,' Devon remarked. Turning to Aunt Sarh he added, 'Aunt Sarh you did say you liked to watch television what you used to watch? You remember the show you used to watch? I wish I had a television.'

'There was some really nice shows sometimes,' Uncle Dolphus answered. 'You remember *The Fugitive* Sarh!'

Aunt Sarh laughed. 'Poor Richard Kimble. The man never killed his wife yet every week that Inspector Gerard hunting him like when you hunting manicou. While the Inspector running behind him, he running behind a one-hand man. That show was on for a long long time. When they took it off I missed Kimble, although I was glad he catch up with the person who killed his wife and cleared his name.

'There was *Coronation Street*. Twice a week it on the television. If Sarh had to go somewhere she making sure she back in time to watch that show. These people used to spend more than half their life in the pub.'

'Aaaye Mr Alvar you think all you could drink down here is these people and them that could drink. Mind you their drink not strong like the rum here. But every night, every day they in the pub. In this *Coronation Street* the pub was like the church. There was like Maran, a little village. Every body know every body business. Every body minding everybody else business.'

'How you mean Aunt Sarh? I didn't know England people have time to mind people business. I thought they too busy.'

165

'What you talking about Dorothy? You don't hear you aunty say how they does peep behind the curtain? Not letting anybody see them but they worse than the police. Was in *Coronation Street* to hear people business. You remember Ena Sharples!' Uncle Dolphus turned to Aunt Sarh.

Aunt Sarh burst out one laugh. 'Lord; Ena Sharples and her hairnet. No matter how Ena dress up she still wearing she hairnet. Just like that other one with she apron.'

'Oh you mean Hilda Ogden, but Hilda was a cleaner. I could hear her singing now. Either singing or quarrelling with her husband.'

'Hilda and Stan. Poor Stan. One day he wanted to surprise Hilda take himself and paint over her picture in the living room.'

'You mean she mural!' Plam, Uncle Dolphus clap his hands. 'Lord she almost kill the man. He had to make sure he had it painted over. Aaaye these people used to make you laugh. Hilda, Ena, Len, Elsie, all of them.'

'You remember them good oui Dolphus! How they called Ena friends again. You know the ones she used to sit in the corner with drinking she pint of stout? That's all she use to drink. Nothing else, just stout.'

'That was eh Minnie; Minnie Caldwell and Martha. That's them Minnie and Martha; Ena used to insult these two women still every night they together. That woman was like a dragon. Her tongue lord talking about somebody tongue that don't have bone was that woman. Anything she had to say she telling it straight straight. I used to feel sorry for Minnie, she so kind of sofy sofy. As soon as she opened her mouth Ena jumped at her making her look small. Well Enaaa . . .' Uncle Dolphus mimicked. 'That's all you hear her saying, "Well Enaa".'

166

'Poor Minnie. She used to suffer under Ena. Not just her, everybody in the Street 'fraid Ena Sharples' mouth.'

Aunt Sarh and Uncle Dolphus started talking to each other as if they forgot we were there with them. Aunt Sarh face sort of shining. Was usually like that when she talking about the television.

'The only person that didn't 'fraid Ena was Elsie Tanner,' Aunt Sarh continued. 'Lord these two women used to argue. They used to beat a combust. Elsie was a sweet woman, and that used to annoy Ena. Every time Elsie bring a new man in the street that set Ena off. Elsie used to tell her how she damn farse, only they don't say "farse". They say . . .'

'Nosey,' I added.

Everybody laughed. 'Aaye aye Dorothy I didn't know you come out in England,' Mr Joe teased me.

'Sarh loved she *Coronation Street*,' Uncle Dolphus added, 'she never missed one programme. She loved Annie Walker and her husband Jack.'

'Jaaack Lloove! Yes dear!' Aunt Sarh kind of closed her mouth to speak. 'Every turn the poor man made Annie called him "Jack love do this", "Jaaack love do that", and he self never said no, only "yes dear" or "yes Annie", and he right behind her. No wonder he died when he died. She pestered the man to go down in the cellar and tout up crate of drinks when she knew he wasn't well.'

'He dead!'

'He dead, yes. Everybody said that was she that killed him. She nagged the poor man too much. You think I letting any woman send me to me grave with her mouth?' Uncle Dolphus glanced at Aunt Sarh as he said that.

'Chupes; people too stupid. Annie was miserable but she loved she Jack . . . she loved she Jack.'

Uncle Dolphus stretched across, brushed his hand across

167

his wife's back. 'Yes Annie loved her Jack and you!' They looked at each other. For a moment everybody else on the verandah became invisible. Then remembering they were not alone they looked away.

The men topped up their glasses. Me, Aunt Sarh and Devon poured out the last of the juice. The sun was on the last leg of its journey through the sky. The day was almost over. Almost, not quite.

'Dorothy what we having tonight? The food in the pot enough for you, Desiree and Devon. You uncle could have something light. Eh Dolphus,' Aunt Sarh turned to Uncle Dolphus. 'You don't want the heavy food again tonight.'

'Anything, anything. You have time to make a bully bakes. I feel like eating a good piece of bully bakes and saltfish.'

'Aaaye look at my trouble nuh. You say you will eat anything and the same time talking about bully bakes. I don't know if I have enough flour. Devon could run in Gouyave and get some. You think you could make Gouyave and come back and bring in the animals before night Devon?'

'Never mind never mind about the bakes I'll have anything you make.'

'Aye aye my uncle look as if he making baby,' I teased. 'Last week he wanted tannia porridge, today he asking for bully bakes. Next thing he go start asking for sour mango and green golden apple. Aunt Sarh watch him you know,' everybody laughed.

'You want me to go in Gouyave and buy the flour,' Devon turned to Aunt Sarh.

'Don't worry. Tomorrow Dorothy could bring up some shopping when she coming up. There is some cornmeal in the cupboard. I'll make some porridge. I wanted it to cook a coo-coo later in the week but I'll use a little bit. Talking about coo-coo that remind me, Desiree, go and pick some

168

okra for your mother. Since last week she asked for some. The short trees below the breadfruit tree in the corner by the boundary with Mr Joe should have enough pick on them. Pick them and bring them down when you going home. Devon before you bring in the animals peel a coconut for me to put in the porridge.'

'Yes. Aunt Sarh tell us what else you used to watch on the television. I like to hear.'

'You that Devon that's all you fit for. You think Aunt Sarh don't have nothing do but tell you about England eh. You think everybody is you. Every minute you want to hear about England England. Why you don't go in England! Why you don't tell Tanty Lucy to send you in England?'

'Bunjay you these two children don't tired quarrel. Dog and cat does behave better that the two of you one flesh and blood.'

'I didn't say nothing you know cousin Dorothy. I just ask Aunt Sarh about the television show and that Desiree start on me with she mouth like alpagat.'

'Come on behave all your self. Devon don't forget to pull some water grass for the pig when you bring them in.'

'Yes Uncle Dolphus. Eh Aunt Sarh what else you used to watch?' Devon persisted.

'Well there used to be *Crossroads* with Meg Richardson, David Hunter, Sandy Richard and Miss Diane.'

'Lord Sarh you could remember thing yes. Look how long they take out *Crossroads* on the telly and you still remember them. David, Meg and Benny. Benny just like McDowell.'

'You mean he stupid!'

'McDowell not stupid. If you think he stupid try to give him wrong change when he buy thing from you, or when he sell you his jacks try to give him wrong money . . . just

169

try. Those people that think he stupid, more stupid than him let them stay dey,' I defended the man.

'Sarh you could really remember things you know. Look how long they finish *Crossroads*,' Uncle Dolphus repeated.

'You don't forget show like that . . . people like Benny and Miss Diane. There was this other show I think even before *Crossroads*. Dolphus you remember. Was this old woman and she family living somewhere in the country in America.'

'Em em,' Uncle Dolphus scratch his head. 'You mean the one when it start the old woman run outside dancing, holding up she frock showing she petticoat and calling she son?'

'Yes, that's the one. She had a grandson and granddaughter too. What it call again? Granny used to dance. What it was? They used to work land planting cultivation and look after animals, and one day the son dig up oil, so from poor poor people they became very rich. The bank manager encouraged them to leave their country house and move to the posh area where the money people lived. Granny didn't want to move. In the end she moved with all her furniture even the animals. She used to make me laugh.'

'*Beverley* . . . *Beverley* something or the other. *Beverley Hillbillies*, that's it, *The Beverley Hillbillies*. I could see granny now. That old woman was funny,' Uncle Dolphus laughed. 'She was something. When she thought was time for her granddaughter to married she used to invite young men in the house and question them. Eeemh. There was that other one where the men moved cattle from one part to another. There always used to end up fighting with men who wanted to thief the cattle. When fight break out their cook always in it.'

'Oh you mean old Wishbone. That was the cook name Wishbone. I don't remember what the show called. While the men cuffing down each other Wishbone coming with his frying pan, stand up on the side and aim good good, and whoop phloop the frying pan land in someone head. Lord we see things on the television yes. It good and bad at the same time. Some things I don't think they should put on especially in front children.' Aunt Sarh went quiet for a while. I looked at her and all of a sudden as if a veil covered her face. Her eyes became watery as if she fighting something in her brain, something sad.

'Aunt Sarh you awright!' I moved closer to her.

She shake her body as when you suck sour golden apple and it seize your teeth.

'Heh Lord, eee Lord have mercy on us,' she mumbled.

Uncle Dolphus looked at her, 'You thinking about the invasion again don't you Sarh? I could always tell. Every time we talk about television she always remember that.'

'The invasion Uncle Dolphus! You don't mean our little war when the Americans came!'

'That time self Dorothy . . . that time self,' Uncle Dolphus answered.

'Lord that was a time for us oui. That was a time in this little Grenada,' Mr Alvar murmured as if he was just waking up. 'You was still in England that time. You see it on the television too?'

Aunt Sarh shook her head. 'When I look and see these people jumping over that wall like animals. Jumping for their lives and realising is my own people. Could be my own family . . . my own flesh and blood, my own people jumping over the wall, jumping for their life,' she repeated over and over, tears streaming down her face.

'Oooom . . . heoomp . . . oooomp . . . ooooo,' Mr Joe groaned.

'Sarh took it bad man, really bad,' Uncle Dolphus mumbled.

I hugged my aunt tightly. Her body was shaking like a child crying for its mother. 'Never mind, Aunt Sarh, never

171

mind. It's over now. Let us pray something like that never happen in Grenada again . . . never,' I comforted her.

Hooooish, Aunt Sarh draw up her nose. She continued, 'Dorothy, Mr Joe, the first time I heard what going on my belly started to run. Run run like I take epsom salts. I spend the whole whole time in the toilet. I phoned the embassy. They couldn't tell me anything. They say they don't know more than what on the television because all telephone link with the island cut off. Lord my head hurt, my belly hurt, my feet hurt. When the big thing break out was then I had pain. There was that radio programme on at the time for black people. The man that ran the programme was a Grenadian, he spend the whole evening talking about what going on at home. People phoning in and talking and things like that and in the background all you hear is that mournful music like when people dead. All I could think of was all these people gone, perhaps the whole of Grenada gone and we don't know. The next day I went to work I couldn't do a thing. All I could see in front of me was people jumping over the wall. Jean, that was a white friend at work, was very good to me. I don't know how many cups of tea she tried to make me drink that day.'

'When I came home that evening I saw my wife she looked as if she sick for months,' Uncle Dolphus took up the story. 'She looked so weak and dull. All she doing was crying and saying that all she family dead. She kept on repeating "all that gun, all that gun. Over the wall, over the wall they jumping trying to save their life." At one time I was thinking of calling the doctor for her. Lord; Dorothy, eh eh that was something. We were not home but I tell you we felt it, we suffered too. One time Sarh started talking about her coconut tree in Boawden.'

'Coconut tree. What coconut tree?' I looked from my uncle to my aunt.

'The coconut tree where she navel string bury. She on about if they mash down the tree she won't find she navel string. She don't belong to anywhere. She always used to tell people about where her navel string bury. Saying that is where her mother registered her as belonging to somewhere. She is a somebody.'

'How you mean I is a somebody? Some people when they leave their country as if they throw stone behind their back. Perhaps their mother burned their navel string so they don't belong anywhere; me, I sure mine bury under short coconut tree in Boawden below the sapodilla tree in my godmother piece of land,' Aunt Sarh emphasised.

Poor Aunt Sarh, I thought. She so far and still thinking about the little things we do. They still matter to her even after all those years in a big country.

'I wanted to come home the same time, didn't I Dolphus? Wanted to catch plane and come home to be with whatever of my family left. We were planning to come home but wasn't ready yet but at that time I just wanted to come ... Lord all that gun. Papa Bunjay I pray I pray. You see these two knees how they white like angel gown, all cream I put on them they still white is white knee I get from praying so that time. Ah fus I pray I get white knee for life.'

Everything went quiet. For once Devon had no question, no comment. It seemed that everyone was scared to speak at that moment in case things started up again. Or could be everyone was deep in their own thought of that dreadful time.

'You hearing about all these other countries fighting fighting,' Uncle Dolphus broke the silence. 'Everyday somewhere in the world they fighting but you don't expect to see that kind of thing happening in your own place, not so, not in a

173

quiet little place like Grenada. You watching the television quite in England at these terrible things happening to your people and you can't do anything.'

'The worst thing eh was nobody couldn't phone home . . . no line . . . no connection. Was about three days later early early in the morning when cousin Annette managed to get through, then phoned me to say all you all right. Dorothy, I know Annette was telling the truth but I had to hear somebody voice myself, so I phoned. I think after that I spent about the next half hour straight straight in the toilet. Like the mess wouldn't stop. It just poured out as when you empty a bucket.'

Since Aunt Sarh came home many times we talked about the 'little war' but I never remembered seeing her so shaken up. You could see the pain in her eyes, feel it in her body. She once said she thought the worse part was not being home with us. I could just imagine.

Quietness again. Bingo whinged. Lappa sneezed. Aunt Sarh shifted in the chair; kind of change the side of her bottom. Uncle Dolphus got up stretched his legs, scratched his head and sat down. Mr Alvar and Mr Joe as though rehearsed eased their bottoms off the seat, rubbed the left leg and settled again. I braced my back against the wall and watched the performance. They were like that little man with the bowler hat and umbrella who used to be on in the theatre, doing all kinds of funny things, making people laugh without saying anything only now there wasn't anything to laugh about.

15

The day was slowly closing its door. The early evening buses were starting to go up. The road was alive. 'Evening Miss Dolphus.' 'Howdy Mr Dolphus.' 'Mr Alvar oye you spend the whole day with you neighbour.' 'Aye aye Mr Joe I don't know when I see you.' The greetings from the people passing along the road went on and on. Buses hooted their horns, cars peep a peep peep. The passage on the sea was beginning to be operative. The fishermen were coming in one by one. Soon the island hopper with steelband blasting would be making its way to St Georges from Carriacou and Petit Martinique. Life went on and on at its meandering pace.

'Lord that morning when Sarh finished talking on the phone was then she bawled. I tell you my lady bawled, she bawled I thought she was going mad,' Uncle Dolphus again broke the silence.

'Aye aye I bawl oui. How you mean? I bawling and praying, thanking God at the same time.'

'That was a time, that was a time,' Mr Alvar stressed. 'We make history. We always making we own history but that was something else. I expect the whole world was looking at us if it on television. Everybody eye on little Grenada. Some people never hear the name before.'

'When they heard the Americans involved that made them

175

more interested. Watching, waiting, waiting, watching,' Uncle Dolphus raised his voice all of a sudden, vex with somebody or the other.

'People funny, was not the first time they hear about Grenada on the television but they don't remember,' Aunt Sarh started again.

'When?' Devon turned his head yeug to face Aunt Sarh.

'The time when we win the Miss World contest. I don't remember what year but . . .'

'Woye o yoye,' Uncle Dolphus clapped his hands. 'Woye o yoye that night you'd think was my wife win beauty contest. Sarh jumped, she danced, she danced. I never see her so happy.'

'How you mean, she must feel good. She must feel real good to see she people winning beauty show,' Mr Joe like he wake up. 'And the girl come from right here you know. Right here in Victoria. All Grenadian must felt good that time.'

'That night before my head hit the pillow I dreaming about home. I was so happy,' Aunt Sarh face brightened up. Memories shifted. 'I used to watch Miss World contest every year. I liked watching the girls from all the different countries. Some of them I don't know why they leave their country, they don't pretty, they don't have common sense. Anyway that year when I hear there was a Miss Grenada I didn't want to miss anything. I finished my housework quick quick and plam myself in front the television. We were living on Balls Pond Road at that time close to the grocery shop run by a little old woman called Minnie. Minnie could drink. Every Sunday morning you see Minnie come out of the pub drunk. How she drink so she curse bad word. She staggering while her poor husband fighting to get her home. There was a barber shop and a betting shop around there too.

'Right outside the grocery shop was a bus stop. I tell you

176

I see something you know. I noticed a blind man used to wait at the bus stop every evening. Just standing in the corner like he waiting for somebody. One evening I came out of the shop just as a 38 bus pulled up, was then I noticed a blind woman with her white stick got off the bus. As she got off the man said "Is that you?" she answered "Is that you?", then they tapped the white stick towards each other, took each other hands and went home. I went in the shop to buy a bread and mentioned it to Minnie was then she told me that the man always waited for his friend to take her home. He takes her to her home in Mildmay Road make sure she inside then tap his way back down Southgate Road. I tell you God give everybody their own wisdom. Although these people can't see anything still they could move about, go to work and help each other.

'What happened the time Miss Grenada win eh Aunt Sarh?' Desiree asked.

'Aaye aye that I telling you about . . . Lord my poor brain start with one thing and go into something else.'

I glanced at my aunt. For a second I almost saw her brains working. This thing inside her head. I think it must look like cold thick cornmeal porridge. It not stiff like coo-coo but too thick to pour out so it settle in the cup. It sort of shaky shaky. Shaky and spongy.

'As I was saying, I finished my work quick and plam myself in front the tele. Wesley that used to work with Dolphus was by us that evening. When the result started coming out my eyes poked on the screen so.'

'Nobody could say a word. Everytime poor Wesley opened his mouth Sarh shush him.'

'I didn't want to miss anything aaaye. When I see she reached the last seven my belly started gripping me. I started sweating. When the man started reading the final three. I

177

didn't hear about third and second. When he said "Miss World 1969" is Miss, and he stopped a little, "Grenada" I jumped up. I screamed. I think was 1969, the brain not all that good now.'

'Lord I don't know how people didn't call police for me that night. I don't know how they didn't report me. The scream Sarh screamed people would think was I beating her.'

'Bawl; how you mean? I jump up in that house . . . jump up and bawl and dance. There was a Jamaican couple living in the flat upstairs. When I bawled out the woman ran downstairs to find out what wrong with me. She was watching the television as well but she didn't remember I was from Grenada. That time I bawling and dancing, dancing from one room to the other. After Miss Lyndsey came down Mr Lyndsey came with a bottle of Captain Morgan and Dolphus took a bottle of Bacardi. Wesley went out to the pub for some more beer and a bottle of sherry for me and Miss Lyndsey. We drank the strong but they said the sherry was for ladies. I had some fried chicken in the kitchen; Miss Lyndsey put on some rice. Quick quick we ruffle up some food and we celebrated. Was a good thing was a Friday night. First time I ever know I drink to drunk.'

'Em emeem,' Uncle Dolphus cleared his throat, glanced at his wife. 'First and only time I had to take out she clothes and put her to bed. My lady gone, she gone.'

'Dolphus behave yourself. I wasn't that drunk. You like to make up things too much. I was a bit tipsy, not that drunk. But I tell you I felt big. I mean when the "Miss Grenada" came out of his mouth Grenada was bigger than England. I mean bigger than the whole of England. That's how I felt.'

'Tell them how Minnie and the others started calling you Miss Grenada eh. All the shopkeepers around started calling her Miss Grenada.'

'How that happen? You tell them you from Grenada?' Devon again.

'Saturday morning I went in the shop that time my head big. The man from the barber shop and the other one from the betting shop was at Minnie when I went in the shop. Minnie asked me if I saw the show before I could open my mouth the man from the betting shop, I think he was from South Africa, a white man from South Africa, anyway before I opened my mouth he asked "Where is this Grenada? I never heard about that place. Must be some little banana republic. Not even on the map." When they say "banana republic" is look down they looking down on us you know.'

'Bunjay oye didn't you pepper his skin? Damn farse. How he mean we not on the map? The man doh damn farse with himself.'

'Ha ha ha hee hee,' Uncle Dolphus burst out one laugh. 'If she pepper his skin Mr Alvar. You see Sarh quiet you think she easy with her mouth when she ready.'

'Mr Joe, Mr Alvar, when he said that I forget what I went in the shop for and I give that man and the others a lesson. I give them a geography lesson. I give them a history lesson. I give them a Grenada-is-the-sweetest-island-in-the-Caribbean lesson. I even draw a map for them. I take one of Minnie brown paper bag and draw the map of Grenada for them show them exactly where I come from and where Miss World come from. It was November so it was cold when I finished with them they were feeling the hot Caribbean sun burning their heads.'

'Woye o yoye,' Mr Joe clapped his hands. 'I could just see you Miss Dolphus. I could see you putting these people in their place.'

'Aaye aye how you mean? These people and them talking to you good good but as soon as they get a little chance they

179

insulting you and think you don't know is insult they insulting you. I put them in their place that morning. Make them know we small but we big. From that day until we moved from that address Minnie and her husband never called me anything else but Miss Grenada.'

Mr Alvar got up, stretched. One thing that does annoy me about that man he always stretching his laziness on people. Stretching and scratching himself at the same time.

'Mr Dolphus I spend the whole day with you. I making a move, making a move before the lady throw my bed outside,' he joked.

'Tell Miss Mabel good night for me eh. And tell her I say thanks for the fish.'

'That's all right. Anytime we get any good grains of jacks you know you'll get some. He stepped over Lappa, started up the steps. Halfway up he turned back and said in a teasing kind of way. 'Goodnight Miss Grenada. I must remember to tell Mabel that story . . . Miss Grenada eh.'

'Miss Grenada. Yes. How you mean?' I answered. 'These people and them too damn farse. She put them in dey place. They think we easy nuh. They think we making joke.'

Uncle Dolphus got up. Shook his legs . . . scratched his head . . . leant over the verandah overlooking the sea. His jawbone twitched as the eyes scanned the horizon.

He chuckled. 'Sarh oye,' he called. 'Sarh, I just thinking . . . Let's go in England for a holiday.'

'Meee. Me saye saye. You go if you want. Any snow I taking in my head now have to fall in Grenada. You good dey oui. Mee!'

180

The Women's Press is Britain's leading women's publishing house. Established in 1978, we publish high-quality fiction and non-fiction from outstanding women writers worldwide. Our exciting and diverse list includes literary fiction, detective novels, biography and autobiography, health, women's studies, handbooks, literary criticism, psychology and self help, the arts, our popular Livewire Books for Teenagers young adult series and the bestselling annual *Women Artists Diary* featuring beautiful colour and black-and-white illustrations from the best in contemporary women's art.

If you would like more information about our books, please send an A5 sae for our latest catalogue and complete list to:

The Sales Department
The Women's Press Ltd
34 Great Sutton Street
London EC1V 0DX
Tel: 0171 251 3007
Fax: 0171 608 1938

Also of interest

Jean Buffong
Under the Silk Cotton Tree

Under the silk cotton tree, Flora weaves her tales of village life.
Of families and friends, strange neighbours and weird events.
Tales of the mermaid on the rock, a sister's death and a father's
neglect. Of pain and warmth, tragedy and joy.

From one of today's most compelling storytellers comes her
internationally acclaimed and richly enchanting novel of one
young woman's view of Grenadian village life.

'Buffong places the reader at the heart of the strong
women whose stories she tells.' *British Book News*

'A wonderfully evocative portrait of growing up on an
island where "news travels faster than African drums"
and carnival is "the whole island together doing things".'
Kirkus Reviews

'Jean Buffong clearly knows the voice of the storyteller,
its emphatic rhythms, its narrative pranks.' Sean Taylor,
City Limits

'Captures a reality that readers from many cultures will
recognise and relish.' *Booklist*

Fiction £5.99
ISBN 0 7043 4317 7